Astral Stalker

Riley Daemon

Author's Note

The following story contains: body horror not involving main character, out of body experiences, astral projection, mentions of past murder, gruesome and violent scenes, stalking, mentions of ritual sacrifice, mentions of past traumatic experiences of a child (including stalking), suicide ideation.

The illustration for chapter ten might induce or trigger megalohydro/thalassophobia.

Sale!

1

Dragons and Dungeons

Deep within the city there was a small cluttered shop filled with crystals and tarot cards galore. All were spread out amongst the many shelves, bringing a sense of tranquility for those who found joy in them. However, the items had the opposite effect for Raina, and she was forced to push down her discomfort. She told herself this was her own hang-up and hers alone.

Raina, with her hood drawn up and hiding behind red-tinted hair, snagged a couple of incense sticks from a table bursting to the brim with them. There were tens of different scents to choose from, but Raina went with the usual; lavender. It was one she wasn't too keen on herself, but it was growing her.

Raina shuffled up to the cash register and swiftly paid with a five before going about her way. The workers on staff were already staring at her from the corners of their eyes. Raina figured they likely found the quiet person wearing an oversized hoodie suspicious. So she hunched her shoulders even further before she hurried from the shop and out onto the busy city streets.

Heartbeat picking up in tempo, Raina's chest constricted with a burning sensation. It was all she could do to try and level her breathing. It would be fine once Raina made it back to her apartment. It was just an issue of getting there. Luckily it wasn't too far as she held onto her incense like a lifeline and power-walked down the street.

'Oh Nick, I hope you're watching over me,' she thought to herself just as she passed by the window of another shop. This one had vibrant posters on the glass and miniature statues lining the windowsill. Only then did Raina come to a stop, distracted as she caught sight of the only image that would gain her instant attention.

It depicted a fire-breathing dragon, its bright orange flames licking viciously at a knight, his sword drawn as they both leered over a captured princess. Raina looked at the face of the dragon, it was slender and spindly, made to look like a monster rather than the animal it was. Raina let out a sigh, *'I wish I could breathe fire too, maybe then...'*

Looking at the knight, her sense of unease returned to her. Then a sudden movement from inside the shop caught Raina's eye. A group of people sat around a table, one of several within the shop, playing some game involving dice and figurines. Around them were shelves and racks full of comics and games, about as cluttered as the crystal shop had been.

Raina's heart lurched as she realized one of the players had turned to look at her, making her next breath get stuck in her throat. Without response, Raina bolted from the window, hurrying the way back to her apartment. Shame scored her because she passed that game store nearly every other day. Yet still Raina couldn't bring herself to enter... she couldn't, it wasn't safe.

Eventually Raina reached the alleyway that led to her apartment complex and once there, she *ran* as if something were chasing her.

'You are fine,' a familiar voice finally echoed in her head. Oh there he was, but she ignored it now, too driven on by the pounding of her heart. Raina frantically apologized for her lack of bravery as she flew up the steps of her building and into the lobby. She only slid to a stop as she gathered the singular letter from her mail cubby; a check from her aunt. Just enough to cover that month's rent.

Raina added it to her cluster of incense as she headed to the old rickety elevator. It hadn't broken and dropped to the basement yet, but with any luck-

'Stop that,' he continued to say and Raina bit her lip. She entered the elevator, glancing every direction to ensure no one else was there before she pressed the button to her floor. The doors slowly closed, making Raina fidget as she remembered the time someone shoved their arm through the opening to stop it from going without them. That ride had been a nightmare.

Eventually the elevator made it to her floor, the doors opening just as slowly. Soon enough, though, Raina was down the hall to her apartment. She looked both ways before she opened the door and slipped inside. Raina's apartment was small, just a singular room with a connected bathroom. It honestly might have been a closet, but at least it was cheap enough for her aunt to be fine paying for it. It was the least she could do for her late brother's daughter, after all.

Raina shut the door behind her and locked the knob along with the dead-bolt. After that was done, she stepped towards the hospital-style bed shoved up against the little nook by the window. Said window had been nailed shut. Raina's nerves still didn't quell as she knelt down to glance under the bed; nothing there. Raina stepped over to the bathroom doorway which had been left wide open, the light still on. She peered inside over at the bare tub, the curtain long since discarded. Everything in the space was clear.

Finally, Raina could breath easily as she went back to the door.

'See?' the voice said, *'I told you I would hold down the fort in your absence.'*

"I know, I know," Raina repeated like a mantra as she put the chain-lock in place. There was the feeling of eyes on her, but this time rather than fright, she only found comfort from them. Even if said gaze was a bit judgmental as she grabbed the bike-lock she kept by the door to wrap it around the handle and tie it to the radiator. The judgement didn't bother Raina, she knew it was out of care.

Still, she went ahead and sat her letter on the small table in the kitchenette, and put one of the fresh incense in her burner on the counter top. Raina lit it using the lighter beside it and blew out the flame to allow the smoky aroma to blanket over her nerves. Raina escaped to her bed to throw her exhausted body onto it, her limbs flopping over as she rolled onto her back. *Finally* Raina could escape from the reality around her; she could go *home*.

The presence around her shifted as he let out a hum, but luckily didn't comment.

Raina's eyes slipped shut and she allowed herself to feel lighter, her body beginning to tingle like static. A pro at this by now, it didn't take long as Raina imagined a rope in front of her that she could grab. Mentally pulling at it with all her might, the sense that she was lifting up overcame her, but Raina's body never actually moved. Moments later, her feet lightly brushed across the old wooden floors, her form shimmering like starlight as she gave her body one last look. It looked peaceful and would stay so until Raina returned.

With a calm smile Raina hurried to the bathroom door and threw herself through it. However, it was not the bathroom she ended up in.

Raina landed on the greenest grass she could have imagined. Rolling hills full of wild flowers and gentle breezes as far as her now-red eyes could see. For Raina had not landed on human feet in this new land, instead she now stood on four powerful silvery paws; and the dragon she was, stood tall.

2
TAKE ME HIGHER

Raina frolicked among the flowers as her short feline-like legs carried her across the hills, sides heaving as the wind rushed past her. She was one with it, giving her true peace. Raina's fluffy tail lashed out, kicking up dirt and grass behind her.

Getting ahead of herself, Raina leaped into the air with the flap of her feathery wings, but she went no higher. Instead, she plummeted back down onto the plush grass, but feeling no pain, she just giggled and leaped back up to continue on her way.

In the distance at the edge of the valley stood a lush spruce forest, a line of vibrant purple flowers growing outside of it. Raina made a b-line for it, her equally lilac-colored tongue lolling out as she imagined herself to be tiring, though in reality she was fine. The world around her flowed its strange energy into her, making each step burst with strength.

This world was the astral. A realm that exists alongside the physical, where spirits roamed free and dreams took place as reality. A realm where you could *be* whatever or *do* whatever.

Raina slowed to a stop as she reached the flowers, lavenders, smiling as she lowered her long neck to sniff at the petals. Their strong scent flowed into her nostrils. She was finally getting used to it after all these years of Nick wearing her down into loving his favorite plant. Raina carefully opened her jaws and gathered one of the stems, plucking the flower with the snap of her sharp fangs. Wagging her tail, Raina took the lavender and entered the trees, going down a familiar path worn down by years of dragon tracks.

Tucking her wings in close, she bounded down a small ridge of rocks into a small grove. Before her stood a small woodland home, built right into the side of an ancient oak. A garden of roses grew in thick bushes around the dragon-sized door. Raina smiled as she walked over to the crystal clear pond off to the side, slipping her wing into the waters. Cupping the feathers, she carefully brought along some of the liquid with her to fling over the plants. Raina watched the dirt greedily soak it up.

"Enjoy!" Raina sang as she moved past the roses and into the cabin. She imagined that a homely earthy scent would have met her as she made her way across the wooden floors. It was only slightly bigger than her apartment in the physical world, but Raina didn't need much space. Making her way to the log table off to the side, she set the lavender flowers on the wood before going into the kitchenette. Unlike the one in her apartment which consisted of modern electric appliances, this one was mostly stone.

With a paw, Raina reached over to open the oven doors, her eyes locked onto the cast iron one inside. She didn't have time to enjoy the whole process of bread making so she imagined the dough already finished. The astral bent to her will and made such a thing appear in the oven, ready to go. Raina smiled and withdrew some kindling she kept beside the stove, tossing it onto the stones at the bottom. Leaning forward, Raina took in a deep rattling breath. Remembering the dragon on the poster, she imagined the blaze as she opened her mouth, but... only sparks came out.

"Damn it, not again," Raina sighed as she leaned back and shut the oven doors. Instead, she just imagined the fire being there and it appeared. "I don't understand why I can't do it myself."

"Knock, knock!" came a deep and masculine voice from the door, the same one that had been chasing her around all day. Raina's excitement bubbled as she spun around to see a man standing there, looking amused as he lifted up a shoddy little basket. "I hope you're ready for our picnic today."

"Nick!" Raina cleared the distance between them, excitedly pressing her hornless forehead into the man's chest, which rumbled with a good natured chuckle. Nick patted the top of Raina's head.

"How's my girl doing?"

Raina simply wagged her tail to show her joy at being there now and it was comfortable between the two of them. Even if he was bizarrely tall at around eight feet, and even Raina as a dragon only went up to his chest. Raina stepped back and looked up at his face, his eyes scarlet just like hers, and a smile appeared on her wolf-like face.

"Just a moment," Raina turned back to her oven, "I'm making bread."

"Delicious," Nick mused as Raina tossed open the oven door, grabbing the cast iron without the need to fear its scorching heat. Pulling it out, she carefully cupped the bread in her paws. As she lifted it up, she hobbled back over to Nick, the man holding up the basket. Raina slipped the bread on top of the fruits and jar of jam before finally returning her paws to the floor.

"Hold up, I got you something," she went to gather up the lavender. Offering it to Nick, it brought a smile to his face as he accepted the plants.

"Oh how kind of you," Nick said as he swept back his long black hair to stick the stalks behind his ear, adding a splash of color to his otherwise neutral clothing. Today he had opted for a short emerald tunic, perfect for traveling in. With that done, Nick held the basket close to his chest and motioned towards the door, "come along, my child."

Raina chuckled at the term, herself nearing thirty, but she supposed that made sense compared to however old Nick was. She just wasn't sure; he had never told her the exact year he died.

The two made their way back out of the forest and through the fields, Nick leading Raina towards the mountains in the distance. It made her feathers quiver as she tucked her wings in close, looking up at the man.

"Tell me you aren't..." she began.

"Why of course," Nick sang, "Raina, it's a beautiful day to fly!"

Before she could respond, he rushed forward, hurrying off towards the mountains at a fast pace. Raina sighed before running after him. Though no matter how hard she pushed herself, Nick was always a step ahead of her. The two bounded over the hills amongst the wind and in no time they were at the foot of the mountain.

Raina slowed to a walk as she looked up at the high peaks, feeling small in their shadows.

"Once we get to the top, we can enjoy our lunch," Nick called out and when Raina looked to him, she found the man perched on top of a rock several feet up. His smile was bright and nearly contagious as it always was, but Raina still hesitated.

"Or we could stay on the ground!" she called.

"Where's the fun in that?!"

Raina blinked and then Nick was even further up. Huffing, she stretched out each of her limbs, giving her wings an experimental flap. Nick cheered her on as Raina reminded herself that this realm was *hers* to bend. She was a dragon! One of the most powerful astral beings and she could do this! Raina snarled and ran forward, leaping towards the rocks. Her paws landed on top of the lowest one and she used it to propel herself upwards.

Raina flailed her wings like a drowning swimmer and collided right into the mountain side. She yelped as she tumbled back down into the grass, for once thankful she couldn't feel anything in the realm. The world around Raina spun as she opened her eyes to see the bright blue sky above, fluffy white clouds taunting that she would never be able to dance amongst them.

"Ugh, why is it so hard?!" Raina growled as she lashed her tail, "It's not fair that *you* can fly so easily."

Nick's face appeared above her as he came down the mountain to look at her with furrowed brows.

"I'm a *ghost*, Raina," he said, "it's like part of the whole afterlife thing."

"So do I have to die to fly?" Raina huffed as she rolled over onto her belly.

"Stop it," the comment got her a small flick on the nose. Raina started and rubbed at the offending mark, mumbling a brief apology. Happy enough at that, Nick looked around the area Raina landed and shrugged, "I suppose this is as nice a spot as any..."

Sitting cross-legged beside her, Nick started to trifle through the basket, passing out each item of food. Raina's small smile returned as she watched him hum and spread the jam on the bread she made. Using a paw, Raina pulled an apple towards her, crushing it between her strong jaws. She savored the juices as they flowed down her maw, except... just like anything in the astral, she couldn't actually taste it. Raina lifted her head back up and accepted the bread from Nick.

Shortly afterwards he began to tear into his own piece, his expression one of pure joy. A flash of jealousy marred Raina's pelt, as she looked down at her own slice with a frown. It *looked* like it should be bursting with flavor, but as this wasn't her true body, she would never be able to tell.

There was a rumble in the air, her *actual* stomach, in the physical world. Nick halted in his own feast as he looked at his dragon companion.

"Ah, you should get going now," Nick said with a frown. It would always seem like their time together was far too short.

"N-No, I'm fine," Raina declared as she snatched the bread between her fangs, greedily scarfing it down without hesitation. Raina licked the flavorless jam off her lips and tried to avert her gaze from Nick's own knowing eyes.

"Raina... You still need to take care of yourself," Nick sighed as he reached over and sat a gentle hand between her two pointed ears. It meant the world to Raina as her eyes slipped comfortably shut; he was right. Nick's voice echoed as Raina slipped away from the astral realm, *'I'll send you lovely dreams tonight.'*

The next time Raina opened her eyes, the world was no longer vibrant and colorful. Instead, she found herself on her old rickety bed in the small dark apartment. Raina's good mood left her as she pulled herself out of bed, her legs feeling like lead as she made her way to the kitchenette. Ignoring the fridge, for there was little there, she opened the cabinet and grabbed a pack of instant noodles. It was a pale comparison to the meal she would have shared with Nick.

Raina's heart was as heavy as her body as she looked back at her desolate bed. She'd have to do her checks around the apartment again and move the table in front of the door. Then Raina would finally be able to attempt to sleep, though the nights were still difficult even with Nick's promise of good dreams. It all hung over her head like heavy rain clouds and she wished she could stay in the astral with him. Nick was all she had, other than the aunt she didn't talk to much.

Raina wasn't sure how much longer she could go on like this...

3

Super Massive...

R inse and repeat. This was how all of Raina's days trickled by. The next day she had to procure more food for herself to which she ventured out into the city again. Raina went to the corner store and bought more cheap snacks to keep her going. Snacks she paid for using what little money she got from doing the internet surveys she often lied on.

Raina would return to the apartment, check the dark corners, check her locks, and then she could go to her *true home* in the astral; home to Nick.

However, it was one of these regular days, the same week as their failed picnic, that Raina accidentally dropped her fork. It was such a small thing, but as she sat at her table with her noodles, she stared down at it. The weight of it all crashed down on her shoulders, making them sag. Heart thudding, there was a sort of hollowness in her chest that was difficult to describe.

'Are you okay?' came Nick's ghostly voice in her head, for he couldn't fully read her mind. Though if she even had any complex thoughts at all, it was... empty.

"I'm just tired," Raina whispered, "I wish to go to the astral now."

'Then I shall await you,' Nick said, though his voice was hesitant. A moment later, Raina felt his presence leave her, further bringing her to ruin. Raina rubbed at her mouth before she left the noodles and fork where they lay; to sit down on the bed with a small creak. Sitting there, she stared into the darkness of her apartment before she fully collapsed onto the bed.

Raina allowed the sense of floating to overtake her and the next time she opened her eyes she was standing on the rolling hills. Sitting back on her haunches, she swept her dark gray tail around herself as she looked up. No longer was the world bright and shiny, but full of dark clouds hefty with rain. That was a first, along with her new sensation of not finding an ounce of joy even in the astral.

Head low, Raina pulled herself up and walked towards the mountain, her tail dragged in the dirt behind her. After some time she reached its base, but didn't dare try flying up again. She was too heavy, always too heavy. Instead, Raina imagined an easy path upwards, and the astral ever so loyal, listened. The stony steps appeared and Raina made her way up slowly.

Once she reached the highest peak, Raina let out a sigh, allowing what she imagined was the thick damp stormy air to soak through her feathers. Raina sat down close to the edge and looked out onto the astral before her. She saw the rolling hills and spruce forest where her home was and even further was another mountain range. Raina hummed, it was almost like a bowl, in a way. A safe little haven she created for herself, one she never went far from.

The astral was vast, but Nick had warned her of its possible dangers should she venture. And so Raina hadn't a need to go elsewhere, except... in the distance, now, she witnessed the clouds shift and move. Something beyond them on top of the other mountain top caught Raina's eye, a sparkle of something dark and unnatural. It was a massive dark spire, practically carved into the rock; a castle. Has that always been there? Raina's tail twitched in a sort of excitement for perhaps exploring this mystery was something new she and Nick could do.

Speaking of which...

"What are you up to, my child?" came the ghost's voice as he stepped up behind her. Raina turned, putting on a forced smile, though the gloomy clouds overhead was evidence that things weren't fine.

"Just thinking to myself," Raina answered, but before Nick had a chance to respond, she motioned to the spot next to her with a paw. The man hesitated, but walked over to sit beside her none-the-less, his legs dangling over the edge of the cliff. The two sat there for a moment with one another, seeking solace; briefly Raina felt at peace.

"Raina, may I be the one to give *you* a gift now?" Nick asked as he reached up and lightly trailed his fingertips across the delicate lavender flowers. In the astral, they would never wilt.

Raina gave a sad smile, "Oh, you don't have to do that."

"I want to, though, as a sign of what our friendship means to me," he went on and looked down towards Raina's neck with great focus. Instinctually, she froze, her mind at a wonder of whatever the specter was about to do. Nick reached forward and brushed his hand across the dragon's throat. In turn Raina held her head back as there was a flash of sparkling light and then a thick collar-like band of gold appeared around her neck.

Flashing lights held the young girl in a daze. What had happened here? The memories felt like an old scar being stretched open anew.

Raina shook off the images that threatened to invade her mind, just as she always did. Instead, she beamed at the sight of her new gift, examining the vibrant rubies that dotted the sides of it; they matched both of their eyes.

"Oh, thank you!" Raina gasped, "It's just like the armor dragon's wear in movies."

"I thought you might like it," Nick smiled as he withdrew his hand. "Just think of it as a way for me to always be with you, even when I'm not there."

A new presence sat beside her, but there was nobody actually there. At least... not physically. These wounds had never actually scarred, had they?

The words made Raina's smile drop as she reached up to glide her clawless paws over the gold. If only she could have such an item in the physical world, but alas just like everything else she loved, it would forever be in the astral. Just like her dragon body and just like Nick. Paws tracing the intricate carvings of the collar, she rolled the thoughts around. Strange shapes rose up from the band; an upside-down triangle that ended with two hooks and a V, creating a diamond like shape.

"What's this symbol?" Raina asked and without missing a beat, Nick simply responded: "It's just a design."

A similar symbol was painted onto the floor. At least, from what she could remember.

And the two fell into a comfortable silence as they continued to sit on the edge of the cliff, looking out onto what was essentially their playground. Raina couldn't help but feel her heaviness and so she leaned over and flopped her massive head onto Nick's shoulder. The man lightly scratched at the downy feathers on her cheek.

"Do you think I could stay here with you forever?" Raina dared ask after a time. There was a slight pause from the other as though he was carefully examining her words.

After another second, Nick sighed, "I think you'd grow tired of me eventually."

The silence was thick with the pressure of the encroaching storm, bringing a rare sense of discomfort between the two. Raina sat up and looked down at her paws, remembering how she'd been feeling back in the physical world.

"I don't think I want to be alive anymore," Raina whispered.

"Raina, no-"

"It's getting worse, Nick," her ears went back as she snapped her sharp red gaze towards his own. "I-I can't keep living like this."

"I-Is there anything I can help with?" Nick went on, his tone frantic, but after all these years, Raina wasn't sure if anything *could* be done. "There has to be something new we can try..."

"You shouldn't feel the *need* to, Nick, you're already dead!" Raina snapped, her tone exasperated. Nick averted his eyes at the words and Raina felt an inkling of shame, knowing it to be a tender subject. However, as he squared off his shoulders, his expression became stoic. Despite all of the years of knowing one another, he was even more difficult to read.

"Please, Raina, you have to keep going..." he said and then his face contorted to one of discomfort, "Your family would want that."

A sharp pain floored Raina that nearly knocked her back into her body, but she remained sure-footed on wobbly legs. That was *her* one line that they never talked about, and Nick had crossed it. Was it to get back at her? That wasn't clear; it was a very un-Nick-like thing to do. Shame leaving her, Raina only felt betrayed.

"How would you know what my family wants?"

There was a long pause and then Nick whispered under his breath, "I knew your mother."

The wind rippled against the two. Raina wanted to think he was joking as he sometimes did, but with such a topic... She knew he wasn't. Nick's expression grew deathly serious as he looked at her, waiting for a response that Raina struggled to muster.

"Why did you never say anything?" she asked past the roaring in her ears, made worse by the hefty astral storm that began to close in around them. In the distance thunder rumbled and Raina tensed at the thought of rain. "*How* did you know her? You died ages ago..."

Nick's scarlet eyes took on a deep sorrow that Raina had never seen before. The man looked to debate something with himself before coming to some unseen conclusion. Pulling himself up, he stood before the one that had been his close companion for twenty years.

"I have not been completely truthful, my dearest Raina, and that was a mistake," Nick said slowly, though his voice remained strong above the harsh winds. Still he looked hesitant, almost bashful as he pressed his hand over where his heart should be. Nick's eyes slid shut and then... from his back, two feathery limbs rolled out in a flash. They were dark as night, but somehow sparkled like they contained stars. Raina found herself tongue tied in awe at such beautiful wings, so much larger and more well kept than her own. But then Nick went on, "truth be told, Nick is simply a nickname from medieval times, for my true name has long since been lost to the ages. However... most know me by the name of *Lucifer*."

Lucifer, *Lucifer*... Raina stumbled back a step and a group of pebbles scattered down the cliffside. That had to be some twisted joke from the ghost, but as Raina looked at his angular face, the way his red eyes looked at her with such worry... She knew he told nothing but the truth. Nick had always been so honest with her, but now... she didn't *want* to believe him.

Before the flashing lights, there was darkness and the rancid smell of viscera.

"N-No, it can't be..." Raina whispered as the black clouds began to swirl overhead. There was a crack of lightning and then another rumble off in the distance, though closer now. Nick, no... *Lucifer*, frowned and began to take a step, before he thought better of it and lowered his foot back to where it was. Instead, he carefully reached out his hand, an offering gesture that Raina could barely comprehend; as if the being in front of her made her head buzz with static. All of her fears and anxieties from the physical world that she never felt in the astral slammed into her. Her chest burned with the urge to flee, but her confused brain at this being her most trusted *friend*, kept her in place.

"Raina-"

"How could you do this to me?!" Raina wailed. More lightning cracked just behind her, sounding like the mountain itself was ripping open. *Flashing lights, flashing lights and sirens.* "I thought we were friends!"

"We *are* friends, Raina," Lucifer pleaded, both his hands out now and pitifully reaching for her as if to show he was harmless. However, she could see it now, his long black nails were actually claws. "*Please* let me explain myself; I just didn't want to drive you away."

Raina frantically shook her head and rain pelted against them. How *dare* he do this to her!

Lucifer looked nervously up at the unruly sky, "R-Raina, please, calm down and let's talk about this."

He was just like the others, he...

"*It's because of you that my family is dead*!" Raina shrieked as she whipped her wings up in defense, but the demon didn't approach any further. Lucifer's face looked as if she had stabbed him through the heart as he stumbled back a step. He grimaced as the first sparkling of tears dotted the corners of his eyes, something he never liked her to see. It was enough to give Raina pause. Their past history flew by her, making her chest feel torn open.

Could she *actually* hear him out? The *Devil*, the one who-

The cracking noise grew louder than the roar of the storm and Raina realized way too late that it hadn't been thunder at all. Whipping around just in time, she witnessed the fragile reality she had crafted, shattering open.

The astral, hungry and vicious in a way she had never experienced, opened a swirling portal of void and space a mere inches behind her. Raina screamed and tried to scramble back, but the black hole was relentless with the strength stronger than a tornado. It ripped Raina right off her feet before she could even blink.

The last thing she heard was Lucifer's frightened scream of "Raina!" before the world she knew best vanished behind her and she whirled into the black-hole's depths.

4

Not, Not a Deer?

Raina's own wails shot back at her as soon as they left her mouth, the space around her echoing in a cacophony of terror. Her body battered and tumbled to the point she didn't know up from down. Until finally, whether it was seconds or hours later, Raina shot out of the violent twisting energy. The dragon whipped through the air, unable to right herself, her wings useless as the force nearly glued them to her back.

Raina, flailing, slammed into a tree of all things. The world still spun as she tumbled down, continuing to slam into every branch on the way down. Until *finally*, she crashed down onto the rocky ground.

As the world continued to spin, Raina clutched her head until the nausea passed. Still, she tried to find purchase on her paws to stand, but her limbs shot out an ache through her body and Raina fell back into the stones. Dread seeped deep into her heart... Raina had... never felt pain like that in the astral. It should have been impossible and the thought of it made the world become chilled around her.

Raina wrapped her fluffy tail around herself as she looked around, her double vision slowly fading back into one. The trees around her were much different than her spruce forest and so she knew the blackhole hadn't spit her out on the other side of her home. Surrounding her, instead, were massive and thick redwoods that went high up enough to caress the endless night sky overhead. It was unlike anything she had seen before.

"I can see the galaxies from here," Raina whispered as she managed to sit up. The purple and blues overhead looked like they were swirling, the stars dancing from distances she couldn't fathom. Out of habit, Raina thought to call for Nick, to get his help and share the beautiful sight with him, but... At the thought, Raina's tongue tasted sour and her mood foul.

Lucifer had played her for a fool and betrayed what little trust she had left in the world. Raina's forelegs wobbled and she nearly fell back down again, wracked with an agony she hadn't felt since childhood. Raina gritted her teeth to swallow back her wail, unsure of what else to do. How could she even exist without him? It was impossible to go back to him and pretend everything was okay.

Lucifer's agonized face flashed through her mind, but Raina quickly pushed it away. It was just another trick of his, the Devil was known for his lies. Absent-mindedly, she pawed at the collar he had just given her.

Raina shook her head and swiped her paw across an ear, she would just go back to her body and then... she didn't know. Raina's eyes slid shut as she mentally reached out towards her body like she always did when she was ready to return. She expected the usual pull in her chest, much like a lifeline, but... there was only empty air. Raina blinked, that wasn't right. Muscles tensed, she tried again, reaching for the rope she used to get out of her body. It pulled back easily like it had been cut.

That... that wasn't possible. The astral didn't work like that! The astral body was supposed to be permanently tethered to the physical body, they didn't exist apart and one was able to return easily and whenever they wished. Raina tried and tried again, but she still found herself in her dragon form on the rocky ground.

"M-Maybe it's the trees," Raina hoped. Dragging herself onto her paws, she slowly began to trudge along. With any hope she would reach the edge of the woods and see what she was actually dealing with. Raina carefully made her way across the stony ground, wondering how the trees were even managing to stay up. The rest of the space around her was also full of thick ferns and vines that made it almost jungle-like.

Raina tried to examine the foliage further, but if she stared too long, the world shifted around as if it were undulating. It made her nausea return and so she just pushed onwards, even as the forest seemed nearly endless. More than once, "Nick's" name threatened to escape from her tongue, but each time she chewed it back. Raina was alone now.

And of course, the worst thing that could happen to someone alone in the woods did. She heard a crunch, like a step being taken towards her. Raina came to an immediate stop, the thick fur trailing down her back rising like a cat's. Mouth becoming dry, Raina dared to look where the sound had come from. That section of forest was now dark and desolate.

A bush rustled several feet away in a different direction. Raina spun around to face it, her eyes nearly bulging and then... a furry brown head popped up from between the leaves. It was adorned with a set of bright red antlers, large black eyes glued to Raina's form. A deer? Raina lowered her tail, fur flattening. The deer tilted its head to the side and Raina wanted to let out a nervous laugh.

"Sorry," she said. "I'm a bit jumpy."

The deer's nose twitched before it moved from the bush, eyes never leaving her. It stepped onto the beaten path with not a hoof, but a paw much similar to Raina's. Except this one was heavily clawed... Raina took a step back as something unsettled flicked on in the back of her mind. A growl came from behind her.

Raina tensed and dared to take her eyes from the first deer to find a second one without antlers, right behind her. Its lips rose up in a snarl to reveal cat-like fangs. Raina's heart skipped a beat. It began to circle her.

"I don't want any trouble," Raina whispered, her legs trembling. The deer didn't respond as the two of them inched closer. Raina was trying to think of a different out when the buck lunged, its snarl echoing through the trees. Raina leaped back, just narrowly missing the snap of its fangs. Raina spun on her hind legs and bolted in the opposite direction. Where she would go, she didn't know.

The strange deer both howled and gave chase.

Raina rushed through the brush and darted around trees. As she ran, she desperately reached out for her body, but never found purchase. All around her, the forest roared to life as more shadowy shapes burst out of hiding. There were *more* of them, a whole herd! Raina shrieked as one of the deer managed to snap at her tail. She lashed out at it, but as she had no natural weapons like many dragons, it did nothing to deter them.

Another leaped on top of Raina's rump, sinking its needle-like claws and fangs into her. Yelling, Raina slammed her side into one of the trees with enough force to knock the deer off. However, another replaced it soon after. Its fangs sank down in the original wound, sending fire down her veins.

Raina bucked as she rushed out of the trees at last, but it didn't fall. Before them was a short expanse of the rocky ground, but... it ended abruptly. Beyond it, only stars were visible from Raina's view. A cliff!

With gritted fangs, Raina tore across the ground towards it, finally opening her wings as the other deer crashed out of the trees behind her. She had to try to fly or risk plummeting; anything had to be better than being torn to shreds. The deer on her back continued to claw and bite.

Just as the other deer were about to reach her, Raina threw herself off the cliff, wings flailing. The astral winds lashed out against Raina's pelt as she spun in the air and sank like a rock. Her scream cut through as she tumbled and slammed into the cliffside, rolling down onto the ground below. She landed in a hard heap, her skull cracking against the stoney ground. The world spun around her again as Raina looked up towards the redwoods to see it fading away from sight.

A great pressure rose up in her head as her vision became dark. Raina tried to find her footing, but couldn't move. The last thing she saw were the twinkling stars in the void overhead before everything went dark.

5

FABLE OF STORY'S END

Y ou should never fall asleep in the astral.

That was what Nick told Raina at the fresh age of thirteen when she finally managed to successfully astral project. Though her memories of the experience were fuzzy because it only lasted for a few short minutes. Raina could recall asking Nick why and him responding that it simply wasn't safe for the living. You never knew where you would end up when you awoke.

Was she dead? Raina pawed at her pounding head with a groan. Cracking her eyes open, her vision pulled back together. Surrounding her were rocks all a shade of various colors of blue. The sight of them and their color gave her a sickening twist in her stomach. Raina may not have been dead, but she sure as hell thought it'd be better than wherever she actually was.

"No, no, no..." came a strange and warbling voice. Raina snapped her head up as she looked towards the cliff she had fallen down.

A deer sat beside it, head held in its paws as it rocked back and forth, sharpened fangs grinding together. At the unnatural sight, Raina pulled herself up despite the heaviness of her limbs and staggered away as quickly as she could. Raina stumbled behind a large boulder that was not too far away, panting once she was safely hidden. Raina's ears twitched, but she didn't hear the deer's pursuit. Raina looked up towards the swirling galaxy above and desperately pawed out towards her body again, looking for any sign of a pull. Still, there was nothing. Raina couldn't help the wet wheeze that escaped her muzzle as the realization sank like a stone into her gut. She was stuck there in the astral.

Either way, Raina still had to find a way out of her current dilemma. The two had fallen into a canyon of some kind, rocky walls going as far as Raina could see. Maybe she could sneak further down without the deer noticing her. Raina took a deep breath and dared to peek around the corner to make sure the creature still hadn't noticed her.

The deer still rocked to itself and then, looking up towards where they had fallen from, let out a wailing shriek. Raina's fur stood on end at the haunting sound, while the deer sobbed and lightly kicked out its hooved back legs. They clattered on the rocks as the deer covered its face back up.

Something uncertain sank into Raina's gut as she witnessed the reaction. The deer was smaller than the others and its reddish brown fur was covered in a mixture of white and black spots. Raina took a careful step back, she should go while it was distracted, but... the cries...

A little girl sat quietly at her aunt's dining table as the woman had a hushed conversation on the phone. The little girl openly stared... had been openly staring as her aunt tried to get her to eat. All up until the phone call.

'You've got to eat something,' said the strange ghost that followed her around. The little girl ignored him though. Instead she finally turned her head to look

at the TV in the living room across the way. There was a cartoon on, one she remembered watching with... It was about a dog that had gotten lost, but now at the end, he finally returned home to his family. The little girl blinked, a welling of tears beginning to cascade down her face.

'Oh no...' whispered the ghost.

Reality was fracturing around her. The little girl lifted her head to the heavens, and finally after a week, she shrieked.

Before Raina could think better of it, she came out of hiding and made her way over to the deer; to the *fawn*.

"Are... you okay?" she asked, though she wasn't quite sure what she was expecting. The fawn leaped onto all fours and snarled, hackles raised. The sight made Raina stumble back a step, but the fawn only kept its distance, weary eyes on her. It was alone now and much smaller than she. *It couldn't hurt her because it wasn't a human, it was a creature, it was a child.* Raina went on to say what she would have wanted to hear, "I'm not going to hurt you."

The fawn's fur lowered, as it naively turned away from her to motion towards the cliffs where the forest once was. Only open air was up there now.

"Herd said never to leave the redwood grove," the fawn sighed. "Astral always changes, always shifts. Will never see family-herd again."

The words, just like the astral, shifted around Raina's mind. As she had left her own astral bubble of safety, would she also never find her way back? Dread seeped down to her core and all Raina could manage was a small, "I'm sorry about that."

Though she knew well enough that such a statement was empty and would bring the fawn-creature little relief. It would end up hating those words just as Raina had when she reached her teens. With that sense of comradery, Raina felt comfortable enough to sit back on her haunches, despite the fact this creature tried to kill her.

It hadn't a heinous mind around the fact she knew. It was just doing this for food and that fact alone was enough to put her at ease. Humans always had much more heinous motives.

"My name is Raina, what's yours?" she asked and that took the fawn off guard as it let out a huff and mirrored her actions.

"Fable of Story's End, child of Storytime and Lore of Story's End," it recited. "But you can just call me Fable, I guess."

Raina nodded before she finally stood and tossed her head back to motion towards the canyon stretched out before them.

"Do you know where we are now?" Raina asked, but Fable only shook its head. The fawn wouldn't be that much help traversing the astral, it would seem. Though Raina decided she didn't care much about that, it would just be nice to have some companionship. While she was used to her loneliness in life, her astral travels were always spent with another. A fact that made her heart hurt. "Would you like to come with me? It'll probably be safer."

Fable frowned, dark eyes never leaving the high cliffs where its family once roamed, "Would you... help find me a new place to live? A safe place, like the grove."

Raina's heart felt heavy for she didn't know if she could make such a promise. The astral had already proved itself to be dangerous, but...she would try.

"Yeah, I'll do that," she said, "it's the least I could do after we both fell down here."

Fable paused and then, "Sorry that I attacked you."

And that was that. Raina ignored the stinging scratches caused by Fable and its family, as the two of them turned to face the canyon before them. The steely blues felt cold and uninviting as they crept along, but at least the astral hadn't yet eaten them as they headed further into its depths.

6

.... The Night it Happened

How long did the two walk that canyon?

Raina wasn't sure as the passage of time within the astral was...strange. It somehow felt far too long and far too short. Not to mention that the canyon itself was a maze of endless twisting gorges and dead ends.

Even so, Fable continued to put its trust into Raina and continued to follow just a step behind her. It made the dragon's fur stand on end as she padded along, for what if the fawn grew too hungry and decided she *was* more suited to be food?

Raina supposed she wouldn't blame Fable, just like the fools who try to keep tigers as pets. There would have been no one but herself to blame. The thoughts made Raina heavy like her very soul was rooting in place. As if the astral had taken her word when she claimed it as her home. Was this some sort of afterlife of eternal punishment? Cruelty was the god that had made her existence to be this.

Raina thought of Lucifer and looked around the deep blue canyon. *Was this Hell?* She thought of Dante's Inferno, but Nick wasn't a fan of the story and kept her looking at tales that were more happy and hopeful. Perhaps just more lies; Raina didn't know what to believe anymore. A realm of punishments didn't seem like the Nick, or *Lucifer*, that Raina had known. Could an entity be so different from how they acted for eighteen-some-odd years? Raina's mind buzzed with uncertainty.

Red and blue lights flashed, turning the night into a surreal dream to the young girl. Sitting in the back of the car she stared off into space, legs coated in somebody else's blood. There was a commotion out there, but she could hardly pay any mind as the buzzing in her head grew stronger. Where was momma? The ambulance had taken her away.

There was a shift in the air beside the young girl and she felt the seat next to hers dip down, though the car doors had never opened to allow another inside.

'I'm sorry that happened,' came a man's voice so tender and fraught with strife. That was the first time she saw him and, even now, wondered if that night had been just a dream. The young girl was far too numb to feel any fear towards him, but she also doubted the police-people out there would allow him so close if he was bad.

The man had long dark hair that draped over his sad face, nearly concealing his strange eyes. They were as red as the blood that coated the young girl, but something about them was kind and brought her a serene calm.

"When will momma come back?" the young girl remembered asking, but the man glanced away, his long fingers fiddling with one another as if lost in uncomfortable thought. When he looked back, he attempted a smile that did little to reassure the young girl, for his eyes were filled with sorrow.

'I'm sorry,' he said again and the young girl was beginning to hate the word. 'Your mother isn't going to return, but...but I'm here for you for however long you shall need me. I vow on my own existence, Raina, that I'll take care of you now-'

"What is that?" came Fable's yip in the present, breaking Raina away from her memories. However, the flashing lights persisted and Raina could only stare as the canyon before them shifted. Along with the lights came the glowing outlines of buildings that looked far more Earthly; a human town.

"Stay close," Raina whispered as she led the fawn along. They entered the new area, lights nearly blinding until they came upon the outlines of the police vehicles. It was a familiar scene, all the cars lined up in front of a neighborhood house. Raina's mouth went dry in her disbelief, "It's my hometown."

"Is it safe here?" Fable asked as Raina fought the urge to step closer to the house. The only way she was able to resist was the squeezing headache brought on by the blaring lights. Queasy, Raina turned away.

"No, we should go," she said to Fable and the two hurried on, a new urgency to their steps. Why was she seeing this? Why was it here and how could Fable also perceive it? Raina moved away from the image of the house to make her way down the mirage of what was once her street. Quickening her pace, Raina thought back to that cool night long ago, running home with a sense of unease.

Again, the lights around her changed as Raina saw an outline of a little girl, running back towards the house, following a boy that was only slightly older. It made Raina grimace as she moved on, examining the neighborhood houses, all dark and unchanged just like the night it happened.

"They never even noticed..." Raina whispered. Eventually they came across the only other house in that town she knew as well as her own. Coming to a stop, Raina sat back on her haunches to stare at it, remembering the smell of pizza from a local restaurant. The taste on her tongue brought back the sounds of those silly Bible cartoons, a dull murmur in the air around her. Sweeping her tail across her paws, Raina wondered if the events that unfolded wouldn't have happened if she had made different choices. If they had just gone camping or...

...or if she hadn't gone over there, when *he* was back from college.

The house and the rest of the lights vanished in the blink of an eye, leaving only the cold blue canyon walls in their wake. Instead of a house in front of them, it was now the mouth of a gaping cavern. Raina leaped back from it as an aura of heat permeated from it like a foul breath that brushed against her. Raina's feathers rustled because if she let her mind wander too much, she could almost feel a sickening gaze on her.

Those stark eyes flashed through her mind. A ghostly pale blue, but the wrath and hatred in them had turned them nearly black. Raina quivered, no, no, she couldn't think of that now. Nick had been the only one to calm her from those visions, but now...

"I don't like it here," Fable whispered as the fawn nervously watched the way Raina shook. Oh right, Fable...Raina shook out her pelt and nodded.

"I don't either," Raina agreed as she took Fable aside and the two continued onwards. Raina wanted to look back, still feeling the eyes on her, but...she couldn't. What if *his* image now stood there? The thought pricked at her brain and made her pick up the pace, until finally the canyon opened up to another steep cliff.

Raina carefully walked over to the edge, looking out onto the endless expanse of void and space. Where would they go now? Raina looked up and around for anywhere else, but there were only bits of floating land and asteroids up ahead. Maybe...

"I think we'll have to cross it," Raina looked down to Fable. Though the possibility of falling and getting hurt *or worse* kept Raina's paws well enough to the ground.

"Will you fly?" Fable glanced over Raina's wings, making her wince.

Flustered, Raina cleared her throat, "I, um, hurt my wings in the fall, I can't fly." Fable hummed as it took her words in, then nervously looked over to the floating rocks.

"Don't like this idea," it stated, but still it carefully shuffled up to Raina and stared up at her expectantly. Raina slowly knelt down before she could think against it and allowed Fable to clamber up onto her back. The fawn's duel claws and hooves jabbed into her skin and made her muscles tense as she remembered the creatures chasing her down.

"Hold on tight, okay?" Raina stood back up, Fable's forelegs wrapped around her neck. Raina attempted to push away her nerves as she looked over the edge of the drop off. She had done far more impressive leaps back in her astral home, but there hadn't been any consequences of falling back then. If she missed the jump now...Raina trotted back several paces before she locked her sights onto the nearest asteroid.

Still sore from being tossed around earlier, she stretched out each limb to loosen the muscles. It would be now or never.

Fable let out a yelp as Raina bolted forward, picking up as much speed as she could before launching herself off the ledge. She soared through the air before landing right on her target. The rock spun around on impact and Raina frantically pawed at it, but her body slipped right off. Raina and Fable barely had enough time to yell as they plummeted. Raina tried to reach out for another floating asteroid, barely missing it, instead landing roughly on a much larger floating platform just below.

Paws stinging, she was otherwise fine as she panted for air through the heavy hammering of her chest. Raina shook her legs and looked out onto the asteroid field as they all swirled around, finding so many more than she initially expected. In a sort of relief, she couldn't hold back the broken laugh that escaped. Raina smiled and looked at Fable who still clutched onto her back.

The fawn's fur looked frazzled, but its eyes sparkled with a hidden excitement as it met Raina's own. Okay, okay, this wasn't so bad. They would be fine!

Raina leaped off the platform to another large asteroid, and then another. She bounced and frolicked just as she would have through the hills. This still *was* the astral she loved, even if she was so far from home. Maybe...maybe it could still bend to her will.

Raina focused and tried to imagine a large rock appearing before them, but the world nary even rippled. Instead, she flew through the air and landed on one that had already been there a bit further down. So much for that.

The two continued to make their way across the rocky belt, Fable howling in what Raina assumed was delight as they made a particularly large jump. Something about the moment, while foreign to Raina, felt almost...nice. Like some emotion she had missed, but it was when she was trying to find a name for the feeling that a dark shadow blanketed its way over the both of them.

7

HOUSE OF HORRORS

Fable's claws sank into Raina's hide as a deep chill crept over the two, cast from the shadow overhead. Raina felt it down to her bones as Fable howled.

"A predator!" it cried, and before Raina could even look up, something massive slammed into the asteroid they were on. The sheer weight of it sent both Raina and Fable tumbling through the vacuum of space between the other rocks and floating debris. Fable, despite its best efforts to keep hold of Raina, slipped off leaving a bloody clawmark across the sides of Raina's neck.

Gritting her teeth against the sting, Raina managed to twist her body, arms flailing out. Raina grabbed Fable before they got too far from one another, bringing the fawn to her chest right before they crash landed on a new asteroid. Raina rolled to ease the brunt of the fall.

Once the two slid to a stop, Raina uncurled herself from around the other. The young deer was shaking, its muzzle buried into the fluff of Raina's chest as she kept a supportive arm around it.

"What was that?" Raina panted as she snapped her head skywards, but whatever it was wasn't there anymore. Only the field of asteroids and distant stars.

"It was a monster," Fable whispered, its ears pinned back. Raina opened her mouth to ask Fable *what* exactly it had seen, but the unnatural rush of wind drowned out anything she was about to say. A metallic screech echoed around and broke the silence of space as Raina spun around, wide-eyed, to see what had forced its way into their path.

With a broken flight pattern, like a moth, a black speck approached them from further away. As it neared, Raina noted that it was vaguely bat-shaped in appearance. As it got even closer she realized with a sickening dread that she was wrong. Raina took a step back as the creature flew straight at them, turning at the last second before it could strike the asteroid they were on. The harsh winds it caused, made the floating mass of land rock slightly, and both Raina and Fable had to dig their paws into the stone to keep footed. They couldn't risk it knocking them off again.

Raina dared describe the creature as one familiar to her; a wyvern. If such a description could be put onto such a sight. Much larger than Raina herself, the beast's scales were dark as night, the same color as the void around them. As it flew it emitted a cloud of wispy shadows that came from the spines on its back. Even through all of that, Raina could see the horrid truth. Those wings looked like human hands, stretched to an unnatural length, the skin on them serving to be the membranes.

Those hand-like wings were attached to a humanoid body, the chest looking sunken and emaciated. The legs had been twisted and broken, to look more animal, the feet a similar way to the wings. And behind it trailed a lashing and spindly tail.

And Raina could not stop her sickened yet curious gaze from trailing up the long neck, the skin of it tinted red from where it had torn away during the elongation. Atop that neck was a massive head, of which the top had the vague indentation of a human skull. Perhaps a remnant of what this creature had once been. Beyond that skull in the dark pools of its sockets, laid its eyes. Starkly against all the shadows, they landed right on Raina, a pale and ghostly blue.

It...it couldn't be...

"We must run!" Fable barked, and finally Raina broke away from her stare down. The wyvern's bloodied mouth twitched at the corners into a gnarled smile, showing off its needle-like teeth. Raina felt like roses had grown inside of her as the blue of the wyvern's eyes vanished, turned nearly black as its pupils blew wide.

With a shriek, Raina grabbed the nape of Fable's neck with her jaws. The fawn yelped as Raina snatched it up and bolted. She ran with her companion to the edge of the asteroid, the wyvern's calls echoing behind them.

Its sharp claws clipped Raina's back as it swooped down, making her tumble straight off the asteroid. Spinning through the air, Raina landed on a much smaller rock, her leg twisting at an angle. Wanting to scream, she only gripped Fable's scruff tighter; she couldn't drop it. Even as Fable wailed and squirmed against her hold. Raina pushed herself up, her back leg trailing behind her as she leaped off the asteroid. She soared through the air before she landed on another one, and then another.

She didn't know where to go, there was no place to hide. Raina was in midair once more when the wyvern rushed at her again. Her head snapped towards it, their eyes meeting, just before the wyvern spun around. Its whip-like tail lashed out and collided with Raina. It sent a painful sting throughout her body as she tumbled through the air.

Damn it all! Raina howled as she was tossed around like a ragdoll. She hated this! This feeling of such hopelessness and *terror*, so unfamiliar to her in the astral. It was supposed to bend to her wills! Raina just wanted to go home, she just...

There was a flash of light and Raina managed to toss her head back just in time to see the specter version of *that house* appear floating behind her.

No, no, no! That's not what she meant! Raina tried to put her paws up to brace herself against the building, but she only phased right through it. The next thing Raina knew, she had slammed right into a beige-colored wall. The dragon slumped to the hard-wood flooring, finally releasing Fable.

The fawn jumped to its feet.

"Raina, get up, it's still coming!" it called and all Raina could do was lift her head to look around. The hallway, though dark, was one that struck her heart with a cold fright, for it was *the* hallway. Raina turned towards the opposite wall.

A picture hung there, depicting an asteroid field against a purple galaxy. It wasn't supposed to be there, she knew. Floating amongst the rocks was a small black speck, but each time Raina blinked, the shape grew closer and closer...

"The picture!" Raina wheezed as she reached out for it, her paws crumbling under her. She hadn't the energy, but Fable understood. It leaped at the offending object, swiping it off the wall with its claws. The frame fell to the floor, face down, with a shattering crack. Now that the wyvern was no longer in sight, Raina was able to breathe a bit more easily, but still she couldn't rest. What if it could still get through the picture?

Raina winced as she forced herself up onto her paws, keeping her back leg propped up slightly. Fable quietly walked over to press up against her other side, giving the extra support she needed. Raina nodded in thanks before turning down the dark hallway. At one point it may have been more bright and cheery, but now it only held a dark and dirty truth.

"We have to get out of here," Raina whispered as she began to shake. "This house...it's evil."

Fable nodded and the two slowly crept down the hall, but as they went further, so did the hallway. The space elongated just like the wyvern's twisted body. Pictures that Raina both remembered and didn't appeared on the walls, making her steps even slower. Until finally, she stopped at one. There was a family picture of four; a mother, father, brother and sister. All but the girl's face was scratched out as if a violent foe had taken offense of their joy.

"What did you look like?" Raina whispered to the picture, ears pinned back against her skull. "I can't really remember..."

The building shook and before Raina could think, the hall broke away. It tumbled downwards, reforming into a set of stairs that lead to a door. The glow of a red light peeked out from underneath and despite the strange ever changing astral layout, Raina knew what it was; the basement. Her voice got caught in her throat as Fable hobbled down the steps to sit at the door.

"W-We can't go in there," Raina said, paws rooted in place. Fable's brow furrowed as it looked from the door to Raina.

"There's nowhere else to go, though," it said and she knew it to be right. Raina's frown deepened into a grimace as she carefully limped down the stairs to sit beside Fable. Its doe-face was innocent enough without its fangs showing, but Raina was unsure if she could explain her feelings to it. She couldn't even bring herself to fully understand.

Still, Raina uttered, "This was where she-" before the door cracked open, making the two of them jump. The red glow bathed them in its light before it finally dissipated and left the steep stairwell dark like the mouth of a cave. The two stared and then like a moth to a flame, Raina was compelled to take the first steps into the basement. Mind numb, Raina wasn't sure why she did it, just like the night it happened.

Something, maybe it was her own instincts or maybe it was Fable after changing its mind, pleaded with her not to go down there.

"But momma, momma could be hurt," Raina mumbled under her breath. Any warmth she could have felt was sapped from her body as an icy chill blew through her. The stairs creaked as she made her way down, until finally her paw pads brushed up against the smooth ground. Raina took a few steps further, feeling Fable's pelt brush up against her legs.

From up ahead came a wheeze and Raina stopped in place. Reality crashed back to her as she blinked, unable to see much in the dark of the basement. She tucked her tail close, draping it over Fable. There was a roar as the red lights snapped back, flooding Raina and Fable in their sudden glow. The two of them winced and Raina expected another new area, but…it actually *was* the basement of her childhood home. And it looked the same as the last time she had seen it.

Raina choked out a garbled whimper as any scream she had got lost in her throat.

The square room before them had dark posters on the walls, a window to the void-like space they just came from. Glow-in-the-dark stars were stuck around here and there, but their light couldn't overtake the red. There was an old tattered couch and a washer and dryer shoved into the corner behind Raina now. A basket of dirty clothes close by, upturned and scattered throughout the room…soaking up the blood. She remembered that clearly, she thought.

Raina's knees wobbled as the memories crashed down around her. There was an old table down there, made of dark wood and carved in a way that its legs resembled roots or branches. There were deer imprinted at its base, and she didn't know if they were like that initially, but now they resembled Fable's family. Their images twisted with their unnatural claws and fangs outstretched, ready to hunt Raina down.

Bizarre items were spread out on top of the table, shadowy crystals, an offering bowl filled with blood, blood, blood. There was a knife coated in it, embedded into the wood. All of it was under the watchful gaze of that owl statue, its wings and talons outspread.

Raina's gaze trailed from the dark altar to the center of the room where a *sigil* had been painted. It was the source of the red glow. A strange somewhat-rectangular symbol with a lot of twisting lines. Raina grimaced because the imagery was seared into her brain.

Thirty-six was the number that rang in her head back then and then an unfamiliar voice echoed at her to run away as fast as she could. Thinking of it again, that one hadn't been Nick...

Raina slowly backed up, but then...it appeared. An apparition materialized into view, but it wasn't a demonic figure. Instead huddled there was the form of a woman. She looked to be in prayer, her long brown hair draped over her face. Raina frowned, her gaze trailing over the dark stream of blood that flowed down the woman's front like a waterfall. An unseen gash across her throat, like a smile. Raina, despite everything, stepped closer.

With the innocence of a child, she whispered, "Momma?"

Just like she had done that night.

"Raina," Fable whispered a warning as the dragon crept over to the woman that continued to bleed out onto the sigil. Raina reached out for her with a gentle paw. How could she help her? Her mother looked up, revealing her face to be an open maw. It dripped with drool and snapped at Raina's face.

The dragon shrieked as she tried to jump back but found the woman's long hair had tangled around her forearms. Fable yelped as it darted away.

"Wait, wait!" Raina called as she tried to pull back, but the woman's hair whipped up to curl around Raina's long neck. The strands were as tight as wire as they wrapped around her, cutting off air flow. Raina twisted and pulled to no avail as she was dragged closer and closer to the gaping jaws of death.

Raina's face was only inches away from the creature's fangs when Fable yelled, "Let her go!"

From the corner of her eyes, Raina saw the fawn rush over, the ritual knife clasped firmly in its jaws. It whipped its head upwards, slashing through the hair with ease. The creature with her mother's body howled in pain as it stumbled back, its hair loosened enough for Raina to slip free.

Holding a wing out for Fable, the fawn used it as a way to clamber up to Raina's back. The knife clattered against the floor as Raina rushed back up the stairs, the basement falling to shadows behind them. Raina threw herself from the doorway, and found herself inside the *actual* house instead of the endless hallway. As Fable jumped down to slam the door shut behind them, Raina whipped around wildly. Her memory was fuzzy, but she was sure the layout was the same.

They were in a much smaller hallway by the stairs that lead to the second floor. The basement door was located behind them and in front was a wall with the family picture Raina saw earlier. Below it was another end table, but looking at it only made her vision blurry, like a texture in a video game that refused to load. Before Raina could try to fight through her memories to see what it was, the house began to shake. A hellish wail echoed around them and the duo knew...the wyvern was coming.

Raina gritted her teeth and rushed a few paces into the house's entryway, hurrying to the front door. She pawed at it with a whine, cursing her lack of claws before she finally managed to wrangle it open. Only to be met with a wall of flesh that pulsated like a heart and blocked her way. Raina gagged and stumbled back.

"Is there another way out?" Fable asked, unaffected by the image.

"Maybe the windows," Raina stated as she bounded through the archway into the living room. Her leg still ached, but she managed to keep it up enough. Taking a step towards the window curtains, Raina hesitated for she feared seeing such viscera again.

In her hesitation, there came a faint blue glow, so unlike the previous red. Raina blinked and tilted her head to look at the picture beside the window. She stepped over and peered at the image. It was of a forest grotto, but the main focus of the image was a crystal blue waterfall cascading down from somewhere unseen. The image gave her hesitation as the color reminded her of those eyes.

Amidst the rumbles of the house, there was a loud crash from the second floor, followed by massive footsteps hurrying towards the stairs. The wyvern was here, they didn't have any more time. Raina grabbed a hold of Fable again and prayed to any god that would listen that this would work. Just like when they escaped from the asteroid field; Raina leaped at the painting.

She melded into its frame and came out of the other side, landing with a soft plop on the grass. The sound of the waterfall met her ears. Raina didn't have time to examine their new area as she unceremoniously dropped Fable to the ground and snapped around. There was another picture there, floating in midair, showing off the living room they just left.

Except now, a shadow stood there with fangs open wide. Raina growled as she kicked out her back legs like a horse. Her paws slammed into the image and shattered it. Raina gasped as the shards embedded themselves into her pads, making her fall onto her stomach. However, she was successful. The picture faded from view, leaving its glass and empty frame to fall onto the grass.

Raina laid there and panted as the smell of petrichor met her nostrils.

For now, they were safe.

8

Don't Go Chasing Waterworks

Raina's back legs wobbled as the glass shards dug further into her paw pads, and the burning pain only increased as she crashed down from her adrenaline high.

"Are you...okay?" Fable asked as it stepped over to her, sparing a weary glance towards the golden picture frame on the grass. Raina opened her mouth to speak, but her throat still felt too tight, like the hair was still squeezing the life out of her. Raina instead rubbed at her neck as she turned towards the grotto entrance where the waterfall from the picture could be heard.

She quietly limped over to it, until the ground dampened and there was a slight spray against her feathers. A much needed breath escaped Raina as she looked skyward; Fable followed the dragon's gaze and gasped.

A large orb floated above them, glowing a faint blue as water cascaded down from it into the small crystal clear pond below. Beside it were bizarre plants she had never seen before with large dark leaves and spindly looking flowers. The area itself had a more purple-hue. Raina dragged herself over to the water's edge to peer down into its depths.

Her own face looked back as dragony as it was, as her eyes carefully slid over to look at her throat. There was nothing there, of course, as the hair had slipped off, but...if she truly looked, she could see the pattern of them appear, like a dark shadow across her neck and arms. Scars that only she could see.

The rest of Raina's strength escaped and she collapsed onto the sandy bank with a hefty plop. Groaning, she spread her back legs out, feeling the glass pull at the skin of her pads.

The scenes within the house began to play in her mind on repeat, except, no...it was images from the night it happened. Raina sputtered and tried to greedily gulp down air, instead sending droplets of spit and tears to mix in with the mythical water.

A great pressure pounded in Raina's head as she remembered a little girl gathering her courage to head down into the dark basement. The confusion and fright of finding her mother there amongst the demonic ritual items. Raina gagged just as there was a gentle tug on her back paw. She flinched back to see Fable examining the cuts. Raina took a deep breath, they were safe for now, they weren't still in there; not anymore.

Raina stretched her paws and allowed the fawn to use its sharp claws to pick out the pieces of glass. Raina winced, her mind ebbing and flowing just like the water in front of her. She had run back up the stairs, running straight into her brother Rory, who was not much older than she. Raina wheezed and laid her head onto her paws, deciding to focus on the pain in them over the one in her chest.

"What was all of that back there?" Fable asked after a time and Raina wished it didn't. The fawn sat down among a pile of glass, done with its task and now staring at Raina with unease. "I am unfamiliar with it."

Raina lifted her head, mouth dry as bone, as she pawed at the grass. It wasn't something she talked about *ever*. Not even with Nick...or, *Lucifer*, rather... Though, he must have always known what had gone down; Raina was sure of it. The betrayal scored hotly against her skin, so much so that she lashed her tail in agitation.

"We were supposed to go camping that weekend," Raina released the tension in her shoulders and slumped over. Fable quietly shuffled closer and laid down beside Raina's belly. "But my only friend, Viola, invited me to her house for a sleepover, so my parents pushed back the trip to let me go."

That was her last pleasant memory, one of childhood innocence. Raina stared at the trickling water, "It was nice, we ate pizza and watched those silly Bible cartoons. I always liked the one with the animals in the big boat."

Fable tilted its head to the side, not fully understanding the human details.

"My friend's family was the church going type," Raina cleared her throat, "but they were nice enough, I guess. My brother was to drop me off, but they let him stay to eat dinner with us before he left, but...he got a bad feeling. His intuition was like no other, so I *knew* something was truly wrong. Despite my friend's pleas, I went back home with him to see what was up. I remember..."

Raina saw the darkness of that night followed by the flashing lights that appeared after the fact. Raina chased them from her mind as she shivered. Fable, having felt it, curled a bit closer to her and...it helped. If only a little bit.

"He ran up the stairs to the second floor, calling out for our parents, but I gravitated towards the basement," Raina went on, nose screwing up at the memory of that damned basement. "Momma always spent a lot of time there so I knew that's where she'd be. She never let me go down there much, always said it was no place for a kid, but...I went anyway and I...found her there, just like that."

Unable to stop herself, Raina lifted a paw to rub at the imagined stripey hair scars on her arms.

"I fled the basement and ran straight into Rory, he looked so pale..." Raina swallowed back bile as her stomach churned. Her current reality fractured around her as she wandered deeper into her mind. "He wouldn't tell me why. I tried to tell him about m-momma, but we...heard something...someone moving throughout the house. We tried to run, but *he* found us and Rory...My brother shoved me to the door, told me to keep running. That was the last time I saw him."

Raina's head hung low on her neck, a deep seeded shame and guilt she couldn't escape encompassed her being. She shouldn't have gone to Viola's instead of camping. She shouldn't have let Rory go back to the house. She shouldn't have left him there.

After a bit, Fable's brows furrowed as the implications reached them. They whispered, "A predator claimed your family?"

"Something like that..." Raina grimaced, "My friend's adult brother was visiting from college. He was at their house that night. I didn't know him well, though he always seemed very nice to me, but that night he was unusually quiet. Then he walked out without a word. It was shortly after that, Rory started to get his bad feeling."

"Why would a previous ally do such a thing?"

That was something Raina had been asking herself ever since it happened. Though perhaps deep down if she peeled back the layers, she could probably pull up some sick and twisted answer. All she had to do was think about how kind Viola's brother had been to her. How invading his ghostly blue eyes had been, but that wasn't something Raina ever wanted to delve into and so she shook her head.

"I'm not sure, Fable," she sighed. "Later on, when I got older, my aunt explained some things. The things I saw in the basement were *Satanic*, so the official story is that he did it as part of some ritual. No one really saw it coming, you know?"

She tried not to think of what would've happened if he *had* caught her. Raina could only hope that he would have killed her quickly. Though as she thought back to her mother on the sacrificial altar, she feared the worst would have happened.

"How does your Viola-friend feel about it?" Fable wondered.

"I don't know, her whole family moved away in a hurry after it happened," Raina was far too drained. "I never saw her again and I never tried to find her. I...distanced myself from everything afterward, I couldn't trust anyone. Except..."

Nick.

Raina couldn't stand the thought of him, but still, she looked at Fable and asked, "Hey do you know of Lucifer?"

To her surprise the fawn let out a laugh.

"Do I?!" it said, "Everyone knows of him! Though I've never met him."

Raina supposed that shouldn't have been surprising, considering the Devil's reputation, and yet it still did. She desperately wanted to ask Fable what they knew of Lucifer, but...the truth brought dread to Raina's heart and she couldn't bear to learn it.

"He started coming around after my family was killed," Raina explained. The pain made her throat thick and painful. "He practically raised me, but I guess it was all some sick joke to him, all things considered."

"Have you talked to him about it?" Fable asked, brows furrowed in thought. As if the idea of Lucifer being cruel was odd to it. Raina's ear twitched as Fable took on a more hopeful appearance, its short and fluffy tail wagging. "Maybe he feels bad about the sacrifices."

"Come on, Raina, you can do it!" Nick cheered with a look of utmost determination. They stood in the hilly fields, not long after Raina had gotten well-enough at astral projection.

*Raina was standing there as a human, a form that didn't quite feel like **her**. When she expressed this to Nick he asked why she didn't just take on a new form instead. Ever since then she had been trying to change shape, but it was a struggle. So many of the forms she took didn't feel quite right.*

"I don't know which one I should try this time," Raina expressed as she twiddled her thumbs. Nick thought about that for a good moment before his eyes sparkled.

"Well, how about something noble and strong?" Nick suggested, "Maybe like a lion? Nobody messes with those!"

*Raina thought it over, but that didn't quite **feel** like her either. Lions lived in prides, and Raina didn't. To be a lion by itself sounded so lonely.*

"I'm not sure..." Raina said as much and Nick sighed with worry. It made her happy, just a little, that this strange ghost cared so much for her. Not for the first time Raina wondered if he was truly her guardian angel.

"Maybe don't think about it," Nick finally suggested after a while. "Clear your mind and let your form take on whatever it pleases."

Huh...she had never thought to do that before, but it was worth a shot. Raina nodded and took a step back. She did as asked and felt herself begin to change as if it was the easiest thing ever, her form flowing like water.

*Raina was pulled down onto all fours, touching the grass with a set of paws. Oh don't tell her, she actually **did** turn into a lion!? Raina's eyes snapped open and immediately met with Nick's. His were wide and wondrous with a hint of pride that was contagious and made her heart swell.*

Raina looked down at herself to be met with the sight of silver and gray fur. She twitched a fluffy tail and when she went to look back at the limb, was instead met with a wall of feathers on her back; a wing. What-

"Raina, you're a dragon!" Nick cheered and before she could register it, the ghostly man so much stronger than he looked, lifted her up into the air to spin around. Raina yelped, but couldn't hold back her wide and toothy smile. "I'm so proud of you!"

Nick set her down then and brandished a golden mirror from his robes to show her a reflection of a wolf-ish snout.

Raina flicked a pointed ear, "What makes this form a dragon? I don't look like the ones on TV."

*"It's your energy, Raina," Nick nodded, "there are many dragons in the astral, and they have all different shapes and sizes. If you met one, you just **feel** it, you know?"*

Raina wasn't sure if she fully understood, but she was just so happy then, she hugged him. If Raina kept thinking about it, maybe the dragon also wouldn't *have felt like her. But in that moment, she was so overjoyed to share it with Nick, that it **became** her true self.*

At the memory, Raina felt a hopeless yearning tug in her chest. She wanted to see her friend again, she needed answers from him. Despite her fears of whatever she would learn, Raina pulled herself up onto her paws. They still stung and the leg she landed on still had a dull ache, but she could manage it for now.

"I need to go to him," Raina declared and in that instant, the sky opened up to bathe the two in a faint golden glow. Fable yelped and scrambled to hide under Raina as she looked up towards the light.

There she saw a mountain, the shape of which was familiar to her. An equally familiar and dark castle sat atop it, and yet somehow the golden glow was being cascaded down to them, like a beacon. It was the same she had seen from the cliff moments before the blackhole gobbled her up. Raina took a step forward. Her sanctuary had to be on the other side of that mountain and that also meant...Lucifer was...

"I need to go there," Raina stated as she turned back to her companion. However, she hesitated as she looked towards the glowing blue waterfall. "This appears to be a nice place to live, if you wish to stay here."

"You can't be sure of that," Fable frowned, "we've only been here for a few short minutes."

"I suppose that's true," Raina sighed as Fable put on a toothy grin and stood up alongside her, raring to go. It brought Raina some comfort as they hurried off, the two ignoring their injuries as they began the long trek to the mountain.

Raina was almost home, she was almost to Lucifer. And she would finally get answers.

9

FALSE PROPHET

A thick fog rolled in, dusting across the companions' ankles; it made Fable keep even closer to Raina. Yet again the astral's reality shifted and a forest of strange twisting trees and glowing blue lily-flowers came into existence. Raina was ready to leave that area in a hurry.

Eventually the soft floral ground beneath them became hard and rocky and the two came out of the mist onto a long stony ridge. The obsidian castle and its golden glow was straight ahead of them. Raina and Fable remained quiet as they took the sight in and trekked along. Loose stones clattered down each side of the mountain, jostled free from their paw steps. Raina's ears pinned back as she peered over the opposite side of the mountain, to see if she could catch sight of her sanctuary.

The fog stretched out as far as she could see. It blanketed the land in a sort of winter, as thick as snow. Raina's heart tugged as she wanted nothing more than to leap down there and return home, but...would it even feel the same? Looking towards the castle, she thought of Nick...of Lucifer and she pushed herself further, ignoring her paws' throbbing aches as shale rubbed up against the wounds.

Raina practically dragged her legs up the grand steps to the golden gates that lead inside. With hesitation, she looked to Fable for reassurance, but the fawn looked just as uneasy. It was now or never, Raina took a deep breath and lightly shoved the double doors open with her head.

A long hallway rolled out before them, held up by pristine marble pillars, massive angelic statues situated between each one. Raina crept forward, the smooth and cool floors soothing her wounds. The angel statues were far too tall, their faces enshrouded by the shadows of the ceiling above. Raina shook out her fur to repress a shiver as the duo approached another set of double doors that held the same sigil as her collar. This one, however, had calcite instead of rubies; a pale blue contrast to the deep red.

The dragon's stomach churned, but Raina would not be thwarted so easily. Nodding to Fable, the fawn tip-toed forward and stood on its hindlegs. Fable pressed its paws against the doors, cracking them open ever so slowly with a squeak that echoed around them.

The two entered and had to blink as the bright gold light was nearly blinding. The castle opened up into more of a temple, pillars holding the top ceiling as the walls gave away to open air. As the surrounding fog threatened to creep in on the room, a harsh wind whipped against Raina. Still she kept her footing as they approached the center of the room. Before them, he sat upon his throne.

"Raina!" Lucifer smiled as he stood, arms wide open just for her. Just as he always had. "I've been so worried!"

It took everything in Raina's willpower to not run into those arms just as *she* always would have. Instead she dug her paws into the smooth flooring to keep herself in place. Raina *wished* she could go back to how things were, but...that ship had long since sailed.

"Why did you do all of this?" Raina called out, deciding to focus on Fable's steady breathing behind her to not lose her nerve.

"What would it matter?" Lucifer asked, looking hurt just as when he told Raina who he was. A sharp sting hit her chest as he went on, "I'm still your friend."

"I don't think friends should lie to each other," Raina answered, "not about something like this."

Lucifer looked off to the side, his gaze landing on Fable. Deep red eyes, once so comforting, set off something eerie within Raina that she couldn't pin-point. The dragon could only chalk it up to his demonic nature becoming more obvious.

"You judge me so harshly, yet travel with an astral parasite?" Lucifer raised a brow and Raina gritted her fangs together, sweeping her tail over Fable's form. The demon before them cleared his throat in apology before he sighed and nodded, "Sorry, sorry, but I suppose you're right. How about we have another picnic and this time I'll promise to tell you everything."

Lucifer had to have been playing with her emotions.

"N-No, I'm not going to let you brush this off," Raina strained her voice as she attempted to put more authority into it. It felt wrong to bring such attention to herself under Lucifer's harsh and burning gaze, but she had already come so far. "You can do that when you accidentally broke the vase in my astral home or when you pretended to forget my birthday that one time, but *not* with this."

"I see..." Lucifer murmured, his own expression as difficult to read as it always had been. It gave Raina one last bit of confidence before her courage dwindled.

"So tell me," she said, "*what* did you have to do with the murder of my family! I...I can't trust you again until you tell me."

For a moment, the only sound was the wind as it whipped through the mountain castle.

"Oh Raina," Lucifer sighed and something shifted and changed. Raina's fur stood on end. "You stupid and sniveling girl."

"Don't you call her that!" Fable bared its teeth, "I don't care *who* you are!"

Lucifer's gaze snapped back at the fawn and Raina further stepped in front of it. Though her legs desperately wobbled as an agony like no other seared through her. It was only the longing for their old connection that kept her standing there and not fleeing like she knew they should.It had to have been a sick joke, it had to...

"Is this who you truly are?" Raina whispered, lip quivering.

Lucifer's expression contorted, spiteful and cruel, "You act surprised that the prince of lies would do such a thing." Raina couldn't look away as Lucifer's eyes flashed to blue, a ghostly color that sank straight into her gut. Had...had that also been him?

"Why do you think he did it?" the young girl whispered one night while sitting on the edge of a hill. Her arms were wrapped tightly around her knees as she stared up in youthful awe at the stars overhead. They danced around and twinkled like magic.

Nick looked at her with a hum, brows furrowed with great contemplation as he took in the weight of her question. His deep scarlet eyes, ones that she once found unsettling but now related to true kindness, sparkled with grief.

"I can't say for sure," Nick sighed, "some people are just rotten to the core and find joy in hurting others."

*"I don't like that," Raina sniffled as she buried her head into her knees. A moment later she felt Nick's firm hand on her shoulder. It was a rare instant of her being able to actually **feel** while in the astral. Nick's hand was warm and spoke of a silent protection, and Raina's throat only grew more tight. It reminded her of dad.*

"Hey, there's still good people out there too," he smiled, though it didn't meet his eyes. "Don't forget that."

It wasn't him.

As soon as the thought struck Raina, this "Lucifer" let out the massive wings on his back just as before, except...the two wings, while black and shadowy, looked more like that of a bat's. They were not the feathery galaxy wings that sparkled like stars.

"You aren't him!" Raina gnashed her teeth and carefully stepped back, finding with a jolt of fright that Fable was no longer there. "You aren't *my* Lucifer!"

"Peculiar," the fake said, voice full of disgust, "you would put that much *faith* into the *Devil,* of all things?"

The way this *imposter* had the audacity to wear his face and speak so ill of him, made Raina boil with a rage unlike any she had felt before. It seared hotly across her flesh and into her stomach.

"He may be the Devil, and he may have lied to me, but..." Raina shivered, "he was still my *friend*, the only one I've had!"

"Vile!" the imposter shrieked as he stomped his feet on the ground, the limbs becoming more bird-like as they struck against the marble flooring. "I could have been your friend! I could have been your *everything*!"

Raina stumbled back as the imposter gripped his head, and a spindly tail slapped against the floor behind him. It thrashed until the image of Lucifer was ripped away, warping and elongating in a painfully unnatural way. The imposter's wings lurched forward and he landed on them, growing in massive size. Raina's breath escaped her as the wyvern shook out its scales and snapped its gnarled jaws.

"Raina..." he said, blue eyes meeting scarlet. The voice rattled around her brain like a hive of wasps as it clicked with a long forgotten part of her memory. The rage in her stomach fizzled out, leaving behind a churning of sickness.

"It's you..." she whispered, "Viola's brother..."

H-How, was that possible?! Raina wanted to scream, for she *knew* the man was no longer living and could astral project. His punishment had been the harshest it could and Raina learned years later that he had gotten lethal injections, but...she knew now that it didn't matter, not when the spirit could live on.

"Yes," her stalker responded, voice deep and echoed as he lurched forward. "I have been looking for you for a long time, Raina. Now, come along, I have to show you something." He motioned towards the temple opening with his snout and when Raina followed the gaze, she found the world around them had gone dark. A putrid swirling miasma was left in the wake of the mountain fog.

Raina didn't know what it was, but could sense a cold and death-like energy permeating from it. It seeped towards her and made her gag. The stalker took another step forward while she wasn't looking.

"Raina, let's go!" came Fable's howl, finally breaking Raina away. Without warning she dashed towards the open double doors where Fable awaited her. The stalker let out his heinous shriek, which shook the astral as the duo hurried back into the hall.

They ran as the pillars began to fall just behind them. Raina panted as she ignored the pain in her paws to keep pace with Fable, making sure the fawn stayed a step ahead of her. They were almost there, almost to the exit when-

The castle crumpled right before them, falling away into the void. Fable yelped and tried to skitter to a stop, but more and more of the hall fell away into nothingness, and soon the two tumbled over the edge. Raina lashed out with her wings, managing to propel herself backwards just enough to reach the edge of the temple that still remained. Her front paws desperately gripped the tiles as her legs dangled over the darkness.

"Fable?!" Raina screamed as she whipped her head wildly around to look for her smaller companion, "Fable, where are you?!"

The fawn was nowhere in sight and as Raina tried to look downwards, more flooring fell away into the abyss. Raina whined as she tried to pull herself up, muscles straining.

A dark shadow fell over her.

"We could have done this the easy way," the stalker snapped as he reached out with one of his arm wings. He slid his claws over her face in a sickening caress, "but I suppose the chase has been fun enough."

The stalker gouged his claws into Raina's skin, and she screamed. They sharply slid down across her left eye to the edge of her mouth. At the white hot agony, Raina released her hold and with her face bloody and gored, she plummeted down into the abyss.

Leaving just the stalker's wild cackle in her wake.

10

He so Loved the Sea

Raina snapped to awareness on a tiny island of sand, glass-clear water surrounding her. A couple of palm trees clustered around, their coconuts spattered here and there in the sand. Raina pressed a paw against the deep gouges on her face, blood dribbling over it as she looked around.

"Fable!" she cried, "Fable, where are you?!"

Raina paced along the water's edge, the white sand scattering with each step. Had it fallen into the waves? Raina was just about to leap in to search when the harsh sound of a wing cut through the air.

High in the sky, the stalker dived straight towards her! Abandoning her search, Raina turned tail and made a mad dash towards the still ocean. Ignoring the burning in her eye, she would swim if she had to, but...Raina shot straight out onto the water, her paws skidding across as if it actually *was* glass.

"Raina!" the stalker howled as he quickly approached. Raina's tail puffed up and she snarled, snapping her teeth, but it did little to ward him off. As Raina sensed him getting closer, she could only keep on running even with the sounds of his howling laughter echoing all around her.

His bird-like feet kicked, claws slashing at her back, but they never went as deep as she knew they could. The stalker was toying with her.

"Leave me alone!" Raina howled, her rage and fright mingling sickeningly together. "We should have just gone camping!"

At the cry, the water beneath her gave away and Raina splashed down. She gasped and held her breath as she flailed, looking for the surface as the cold water seeped through her fur. The stalker loomed above, his talons lashing out into the waves. There was a sizzle and then the stalker shrieked as if the water had burned. Then there was finally silence as Raina continued to sink down into the depths.

Raina could no longer hold her breath and her mouth was forced open, bubbles floating upwards. However...none of the water fought to get into her lungs. Each breath was as fresh as the sky above. Raina let out a relieved sigh as her body grew limp in exhaustion. She had been running for far too long.

Raina drifted downwards, the world above her turning to a murky dark as she slipped further away from the sunlight. Raina tensed as she feared total darkness, but then there came alive a faint low light that illuminated around her. Raina blinked and glanced down to see her collar emitting the faintest of glows. It reminded her of the castle, but...far more inviting. Raina kept hold of its warmth to not lose her wills as the chill creeped through her fur down to the bone. And, at least, it also helped to fully numb the pain in her paws finally.

Eventually they brushed up against the sandy ocean floor. Stretching her paws out, the water wasn't as suffocating as she thought, offering her weightlessness. That allowed Raina to keep on going, despite how drained she was. She just wished Fable was there, worried over the fawn's fate.

Maybe I was never truly as alone as I thought...but now that I am... Her heart hurt for the friendship and love she never allowed herself before. Raina...wasn't sure if she could keep going.

"I never wanted any of this," she whispered, yet still something kept her moving forward. Raina pictured Lucifer's gentle face in her mind, back when he was just Nick, and when his love meant everything to her. The moment Raina saw the stalker take on his image and try to act as him, Raina refused to believe that Lucifer would *ever* hurt her. Perhaps that was a foolish thought...

The light from her collar became just a bit brighter and Raina was able to make it a few more feet as the scenery before her changed. Despite the undersea darkness, a second body of water formed. Raina grimaced as she immediately recognized the lake and off in the distance, the cabin. That's where they would have stayed that weekend. Where they would have survived.

"Are you so sure about that?" came the voice of the ocean. Raina blinked and tilted her head to the side to ask what the murky depths meant by that. Before her appeared a shadow, in the wyvernly shape of her stalker. The creature bore its eyes against her as it opened its massive wings above the lake. From the water rose up the corpses, more than Raina could count. Bile flooded her throat as the bodies went even higher, flying in rapture towards the surface of the ocean. Raina dared step closer and her paws sank into the mud.

Maybe...it truly *wouldn't* have mattered. Who was to say that the creature wouldn't have waited for a second opportunity?

"This is true," said the ocean, "there are many winding paths, but sometimes there's no changing where you end up. What happened certainly wasn't *your* fault."

Raina submerged even further into the muck.

Why had she lived her life like this? Raina recalled the hopelessness, the hollowness of her heart, drifting away with the currents. And in its place she allowed the salt of the sea to engulf her. The ocean-thing that spoke to her was right, it wasn't her fault, it was *his*. Raina lashed out her tail and some of the mud broke away. *How dare he, how dare he-*

Raina pulled herself from the muck and stomped over to the lake's edge, looking up towards the shadows.

"Please help me," she called, "I can't let him get away with hurting me even more!"

Something burst through the ground just below her and Raina yelped as she was lifted upwards. The seafloor was left behind as the pressure forced her down to her belly. She was met with scales and for a moment panicked that it was another one of the stalker's tricks. However, at the thought, the ocean creature blew out a breath that sent an overwhelming sense of calm through her.

The ocean god swam up and up, the pressure of the water easing up and making Raina woozy. Until finally light hit them and Raina breached the surface, finding the calm water was no more. The sea raged on with harsh waves and winds, tossing around the bodies from before. To her horror they were more numerous than before and Raina could only cower against the beast as the rain pelted against her.

"What happened?!" Raina called, but the creature did not answer her, instead it dragged her further through the waves, making her sputter and cough. Eventually she managed to keep her eye open long enough to catch sight of what appeared to be a large rock jutting out of the water. The beast lifted itself up high and deposited her onto the rocky shore.

Raina fell away from it with a pull and snap, her chest far heavier than before. Once she landed, Raina spun around to face the being that helped her, but instead she only witnessed a massive violet sail dipping below the aggressive sea. Yet still its voice was serene as they called out, "Do be more careful from here on out."

Raina wanted to call out to the creature to thank it, but her voice was quickly drowned out by the raging storm. Shelter was a must, some place safe and far away from wherever the stalker might still lurk. Raina took in her surroundings, and there amongst the rocks she noticed a peculiar looking shadow. Bounding over to it, she found a crevice nestled there, just big enough for her to squeeze through.

Raina pushed herself forward and slipped inside, her chest pressing roughly up against the rocks though she hardly felt it. Once on the other side, Raina was relieved to find it much bigger there. Enough for her to stretch out, but in doing so, was only reminded that she was now alone.

With a deep sadness, Raina absently rubbed at where the rocks had jabbed into her chest only...she found not fur, but something much harder and smooth. Raina looked to see that her underside was now covered in scales, much more like a traditional dragon, her gray fur wildly sticking up around it. Shocked, Raina shifted her movements to get a better look of it, it was a silvery-blue and shone like the ocean waves. Such a color would have once horrified her to have as a part of herself, but...it reminded her of the sea. Reminded her of her dad and how he once loved the sea...

Raina leaned her head down a bit more, nearly seeing her reflection in the glow. Her eye landed on the marred side of her face. It was still sticky with blood and the vision was shadowy. Well, at least her back paws no longer hurt and when she checked them, only found light scarring where the glass shards had once cut her open. Raina groaned as she stood up straight, lightly patting her chest again to hear it clang like armor.

"So strange," Raina whispered, but she couldn't help that it felt...right. Just like the rest of her. Raina fanned out what was left of her fur and turned towards the deeper parts of the caves. If she continued to walk, she would no doubt end up elsewhere in the astral and so she continued on her journey. Alone, but perhaps not as her watery scales rippled. Not everyone was bad, she repeated to herself, not everyone...

The image of Fable's toothy smile flashed in through her mind. Oh how she missed it just as she missed Lucifer.

Raina continued deeper into the cave until all light vanished and she was left with the distant roar of the storm; until that too became quiet. Raina's ears pinned back as she tip-toed along, the darkness making her vision ripple. What if *he* was hiding out there somewhere, still waiting for her...what if he had hidden away from the storm in this cave as well?

Before Raina could regret her choices, the quiet was replaced by a beat. A rhythmic thumping that rose up somewhere in the distance like...music? Raina's paws kept moving forward and then there was a flicker and a faint blue glow warmly brushed against her pelt. It made her fur stand on end as she snapped her sights towards the light.

The tunnel finally opened up ahead, giving way to the night sky. Raina bounded towards it, ready to rid herself of the dark. As she neared the crevice, the music got louder and Raina had to slide to a stop just before she ran out. Instead, she carefully poked her head through to check and see if the coast was clear. Raina was met with large rocky walls surrounding the area. The rock the ocean god left her on, a half-submerged mountain she realized, had a large crater in its center that reminded her a lot of the bowl-like dome of her sanctuary. Up above, the night sky was filled to the brim with sparkling stars, nearly bursting.

Raina crept out of her hiding place and onto a ridge overlooking the crater. She made her way to the edge where the music and faint blue glow came from. Paws braced against the stones, Raina leaned over to look and a sharp gasp escaped her.

Down below sat two massive bon-fires, crackling with peculiar blue flames. Surrounding them were...*creatures* of varying shapes and sizes, dancing and twisting around together, in what appeared a joyous manner. Some looked more humanoid, with simple animal heads or large bird-like wings, but others...their forms made no sense, with multiple limbs and eyes, far too many to count, all undulating as they moved about.

Raina averted her eye as her stomach flipped, and caught sight of a ridge across the way, slightly lower than hers. A band of mostly humanoids, were spread out playing strange instruments; the source of the music. It wasn't a bad tune in any way, but it greatly unsettled her, knowing all she had seen in the astral thus far.

It couldn't happen again. The memory of her astral momma's hair wrapped around her throat or the stalker's claws on her, made her take a slow step back. Raina needed to make herself scarce before she was noticed...the ocean flashed into her mind along with the creature that helped her. Raina came to a stop, but not soon enough as her back paw brushed up against something feathery that wasn't her own.

Raina leaped around like a cat, fur on end, only to come face to face with a *massive* eye-ball. From it flowed several wing-like appendages as it let out a curious trill and reached for her with one of them. Raina yelped and skittered backwards in her shock, her foot catching on the edge of the ridge. The creature in front of her looked shocked as one of its wings whipped forward to grab her, but it was too late.

Raina slipped over the edge and plummeted down into the crater.

11

MOUNT HERMON

Rocks tumbled around Raina as she tried to scramble back up the slope to no avail; her clawless paws useless. *Damn it!* She wished she had them now. Raina bounced off the next ridge down, a flare of pain going through her side before she finally slid down to the bottom of the crater. Raina landed in a heavy heap, stars in her vision.

The dragon rubbed her head as she shook the sparkles away and sat up.

Eyes. There were far too many sets of eyes that stared her down. Raina nearly screamed as she scrambled onto her paws, tail lashing. The beings closest to her stopped their dancing, as if they were just as confused by her appearance as she was of them. The rest of the massive crowd continued on with their party, none-the-wiser.

One of the creatures to her left, staggered forward with a weird gate. It was headless and only consisted of several thick wing-like arms, each littered with claws. Raina's legs quivered as the thing warbled at her in a language she couldn't understand; it sounded nearly mechanical. Was it threatening her? Raina shuffled backwards, but her rump pressed up against the rocky wall behind her. Shale from above clattered down as the winged eyeball hung down from the ledge to stare after her.

She was surrounded.

Raina hissed and arched her back to warn the encroaching creatures that she wouldn't go without a fight. She had already come too far. The group hesitated, several of them whispering to one another in their strange language. The one with the many limbs, lifted a single wing towards her and continued to speak. It sounded... like a question.

"Armaros and the others simply wish to know if you're alright," came a loud and commanding voice from above. Raina and the creatures turned their attention skywards and that's when she first saw him.

Standing on the highest peak to look over the crater was a bright flash of white, another creature far too high up for Raina to catch many details. Yet... that voice reverberated through her as the vibrant creature opened up a massive pair of wings. "Allow the stranger her space."

The beings around Raina all but backed away, though they kept their many weary eyes on her. The bright white detached from the cliffside and glided down the crater walls, heading straight for the group. As the creature flew lower into the shadows around them, the blue fire light washed out its own.

Something clicked in Raina's head, almost like a sixth sense going off, and finally she understood what Lucifer had meant. For this stranger looked a similar way to her, covered in downy fur-like feathers. Though his wings were far larger, *he* was larger and nearly twice her size, but still she knew what he was; a dragon. The energy around him bore pure strength in its burning hot intensity, and yet, somehow, through all of that she could sense something else. Like water, calm and maybe a bit frigid, it reminded Raina of when lava hit the ocean, creating something of a sturdy rock from it.

Is this what Lucifer felt when he saw me as a dragon? He had this much faith in me being strong?

Not having enough time to dwell on it, Raina scrambled away as this new dragon landed only inches from where she previously stood. His paws graced the stones with ease, claws clacking with a pleasing sound. The stranger stood on his hind-legs for a moment, wings flared and chest out with pride.

Raina could only stare at the way his feathers puffed out thickly around his neck like a lion's mane. The blue flames made his own blue highlights and markings sparkle and glow with something unnatural. It reminded Raina of the wyvern's eyes and she instinctively flexed her toes to prepare to run. However, this new dragon turned his gaze towards her; he had an angelic amount of eyes splattered across his handsome fox-like face. At first she thought the eyes to also be blue, but on closer inspection they had more of a green-ish tint to them.

The dragon returned to his four paws and Raina's tension eased, though she knew she couldn't truly let her guard down. The stranger motioned at the other surrounding creatures with a wing and they immediately went back to their business around the flames. As he finally tucked his wings in, Raina wondered if it was a good time to slip away while his back was to her.

"So what do we owe the pleasure?" the stranger turned to her before she could, his smile kept her in place. "The Watchers don't get many visitors these days."

Watchers? Raina thought of the hundreds of eyes around her as she responded, "I'm just passing through."

"Well I suppose the lost will wander long enough to find those that don't want to be found," the stranger mused. Raina scanned over him, desperately searching for any sign he'd turn on her, but...he appeared at ease.

Testing the waters with him, Raina whispered, "Actually, I'm looking for my friend."

"Of course," he nodded and finally turned away from her, flicking his long and feathery tail, "come along."

The other creatures parted like waves to allow the dragon through. Raina wanted to hesitate, but ultimately decided it best to keep close to the other.

"There's no reason to fear while you are here," the stranger said as he waited for her to reach his side before continuing on their way. The fire's blue glow and constant thrumming of the music made Raina feel more than a little disorientated. Not to mention the vapid limbs twisting and pulsating around her, though the stranger didn't appear to mind it. They made their way over to the furthest bon-fire in the crater, making a quick turn towards another group of the strange beings.

Most notably, the stranger stomped over to a more humanoid looking one. It was covered in brown and white fur with two jagged scars on its back. As though it once had wings that were torn off.

"Azazel," the stranger announced his presence as he sat back on his haunches. Even sitting, the dragon was at eye-level with the other. The one in question turned around, making Raina leap back a step. His head was that of a goat's, and at her sudden surprise, his red eyes scanned over Raina with a sort of amusement. He smiled and she could see that the goat's muzzle was full of sharp teeth. It reminded her greatly of Fable just as his eyes reminded her of Lucifer's. A sharp pang hit Raina's chest that she wallowed in.

"What's up, boss man?" Azazel asked in a playful drawl as he put a hand on his hip.

The white dragon uttered four simple words, "Fable's friend is here."

Raina's ears flicked forward as she wondered if she heard that correctly.

"My friend!" came a familiar cheer that washed away the rest of Raina's fears and doubts. She spun around and saw the young fawn bounding straight towards her. Forgetting all other concerns, Raina bolted towards the other, her paws carrying her swiftly over the rocky ground. Once she reached Fable, Raina reared onto her hindlegs, arms wide open as it leaped into them. The fawn slammed into her and nearly knocked the air from Raina's lungs as she stumbled back a step.

Raina and Fable wrapped their arms around one another, and she couldn't help but be surprised at how much sturdier the fawn felt. Raina leaned back and saw how the deer's pelt was void of all but a few remaining spots, its head adorning two fuzzy stalks; future antlers. How much time had actually passed since they last saw each other?

"How did you even get here?" Raina asked as she returned Fable to their hooves and paws. She kept one of her own gently on top of its head, its ears twitched happily.

"I fell in the water and realized at that moment that I don't know how to swim!" Fable laughed as if it hadn't been that serious of a situation. Fable sat back on its haunches and mimicked the action of doggy-paddling. "I was drowning, but then Azazel pulled me out!"

"It was lucky we were in the area," Azazel trotted up to the duo. He reached over and patted Fable on the head. "We love having this little creature here, it's a hoot!"

Fable grinned, "And I'm not even an owl!"

"Well, thank-you, it means a lot to me," Raina whispered, unable to find her voice. Looking around to the creatures of the crater as they partied, she realized their strange stares weren't at all malicious. Not like how the stalker looked at her. Raina grimaced, unsure of how to handle such kindness within the unkind realm.

"Watchers don't let children, even weird little deer things, drown," came the stranger's smooth voice as he walked over to join the group. Azazel nodded enthusiastically as several of the closest beings let out noises that could be described as cheers. Raina stared down the other dragon and though he looked not much different than her, it seemed so natural for him to be amongst the strange beings.

"If you don't mind my asking, *what* are you exactly?" Raina finally broke the ice, getting the stranger to blink in surprise as if the answer was obvious. He opened his mouth to speak, but Azazel beat him to it.

"We're angels!" the goat man threw up his fist with a cackle and another series of cheers roared up around him, much more numerous this time.

"*Fallen* angels," the stranger sighed, his tone softer and quieter than Azazel's. Raina's and his eyes lingered on one another for a time. Fallen angels... that meant they were similar to Lucifer. Raina wanted to back away, but couldn't find the will to do so. Her memories of Nick flowed back to her on a stream of memory as she thought of how Azazel had gone out of his way to rescue Fable.

"I've always heard fallen angels were bad, but..." Raina said quietly enough for only the stranger nearest her to hear. Though she trailed off, for she wondered if it was an offensive topic and didn't want to face any possible wrath.

"That's like saying all humans are bad, but I've met plenty of nice ones in my day," the stranger responded calmly. His multi-eyed gaze looked upon her knowingly, "Wouldn't you say?"

She wasn't sure if she could, but...she wanted to be able to one day.

"What makes you fallen?" Raina decided to ask instead of diving into herself.

"Some of us are actually just Old Gods clutching to demonic names so we may yet still survive," the stranger explained to her, but then a frown marred his muzzle as if the next topic was personal. "The rest are just poor souls simply dealt the short end of the stick. History is always written by the victors, as they say."

Regret began to bubble under Raina's skin.

Despite everything, all of the lies and...whether Lucifer *did* have anything to do with her family's deaths or not, Raina missed him. With her heart far heavier and mind full of conflicted thoughts, Raina sighed and made to turn away, "Well, we should be going..."

She had to get home, back to her body and to Lucifer. Raina knew she would never have closure otherwise.

"Ah, so soon?" Azazel frowned before he motioned towards the pleasantly warm fires around them, "You're welcome to enjoy the festivities for as long as you want."

Raina was about to deny him when Fable turned to her, looking hopeful, "It's *safe* here, Raina, we're with friends!"

On impulse, Raina grinded her teeth together, the weight in her chest becoming deafening. It *was* safe enough here, Fable's time alone with the Watchers had proved. Perhaps safe enough for the deer to live there, if the fallen angels allowed it. Raina should have been glad to have found a suitable place for it, but...why did that also hurt? Raina, unsure of how to respond, stuttered and nervously glanced towards the cliff walls for a way out. Should she just leave, or-

Instead, the stranger caught her eye. He had a playful smirk as he tucked in his wings and hoisted himself back up onto his hind legs. With a foreleg behind his back, he bowed deeply, the horns on his head sparkling against the light of the flames.

"Would you at least stay for a dance?" he asked. Raina's fur stood on end and the skin around her nares heated up. She had never danced before, and certainly had never been *asked* for a dance. There was no way she could do that.

As Raina hesitated, the stranger hummed in acceptance when she didn't take his paw and made to move away. With him, her heart lurched for what she had long since missed in life. Wasn't this just something people *did* sometimes? Dance the night away with a stranger you may never see again and perhaps this was her chance to experience it...

Raina's muscles tensed as she pushed herself onto her hind-legs, using her tail for balance. The stranger's ears flicked forward in surprise as Raina reached out. He met her halfway, his own paws warm as they slotted perfectly together. The stranger's smile became more genuine as his claws wrapped around her paw, though they never marred the flesh. So unlike the ones that gouged her face.

Unused to two legs, Raina staggered a couple of steps before stumbling, being met with a face full of thick white feathers. She jumped back with a stutter, but the stranger only laughed in his playful tone...but ever nervous, Raina's ears flicked around to listen in on her surroundings, to see if anyone had seen her fall.

Nearby Azazel took hold of Fable's paws and the two bounced around, their hooves clattering on the stones to the rapid beat of the music. Raina focused on the two and patterned her paws to a similar rhythm. The stranger grinned and did the same, leaning further back just as Raina did. The two quadrupeds used each other's weight to keep themselves upright for if their hold were to break, they would fall. Raina put her trust into him, her wings flailing in a rare joy.

They spun around each other, their tails twirling for who knows how long. The air around them was heavy with the storm long since past. The fires that served as their celebratory lights nearly sent her into a daze, but it was not such an unpleasant one. It allowed her mind to rest for once. Raina practically was in the other dragon's arms at one point as their dual set of paws continued to hobble around. It was warm, she was warm and she was safe.

Their paws locked again as he spun her and she grinned a genuine one. Then sometime later, the stranger dipped her low and Raina could see the galaxy just past his eyes. Swirling and unfamiliar, letting her know she was still some ways away from home. Raina sighed and finally he pulled her back up before releasing her and returning to his four legs. Raina followed shortly after.

Despite the continued music, things were quiet in Raina's mind as the stranger's eyes glazed over her for perhaps one last time.

"Well, truly, I hope you have a safe journey," he stepped around her and made his way along the crater's rocky wall, avoiding the massive groups that congregated in the center. Raina watched him go for a time before she looked at where Fable and Azazel were still playing around, none-the-wiser to her or the stranger. She could leave now while no one was paying attention and it would be easier, but...maybe it wouldn't hurt to prolong things. She was still so curious about that stranger, after all.

Raina followed after where he had gone. Watching as he clambered his way up the slope back to the top of the crater. She slowed, looking over the edge to watch the Watchers continue their party. Soon enough, though, she pulled herself to the upper most ridge, the stars there appeared close enough to touch.

The wind buffeted against Raina's pelt as she approached where the stranger now fiddled with some rocks. As she grew closer, Raina noticed he had plucked a couple of plants unknown to her and crushed them into a stone bowl. He motioned for her to lean closer so Raina did as asked. The stranger lathered his paws in the goo and carefully brought the salve to the deep gouges on her face.

It stung and she let out a sharp hiss, but it soon soothed to the point of no longer hurting at all. Raina let out a relieved sigh and slowly opened the damaged eye. It still had sight, somewhat, though there was a slight blur. Raina took the stranger in with it, but the glowing blue flecks on his pelt were too much, the astigmatism in the eye far too great.

Raina blinked it shut again and gave a small thanks to the stranger anyway.

"Wyverns are toxic to their core," the stranger said as he stepped back and trotted closer to the edge of the cliff. He peered down into the crater, "You'll do good to remember that."

Raina nodded and tossed her head back to look over the opposite ledge to see where in the astral they were. The scene should have been different than the one she came from, but...it was still the flooded sea out there and if she squinted, she could even make out the corpses.

"Ah! T-The bodies-" Raina gasped as she stumbled back. The stranger was quick to stick out his wing before she plummeted off the edge into the crater again.

"They're just an illusion of the past," the stranger said, his tone tired. "They can't hurt you."

Raina worried her lip as she tore her sights away from the bodies. Instead she stepped over to where the stranger was to sit beside him. Ears drooping as she looked out onto the crowd, Raina asked, "Do the others know about them?" It was hard for her to imagine they would be so happy if they had.

"Perhaps deep down they do, but I haven't allowed many up here," the stranger mused. His many eyes bore down upon her, "Sometimes caring about another means shouldering the burden of secrets you know would hurt them."

Lucifer's pained face flashed through Raina's mind again. Feeling like a knife had been driven through her ribs, Raina coughed past the hurt as she whispered, "What if they end up hating you for it?"

"It's a risk I have to take..." the stranger said as he looked down at the armor plating of Raina's chest. How it shone against the stars with the ripples of the ocean before casting his gaze out onto the dancing Watchers. His green gaze was full of adoration for them, "It's what a protector would do."

"I think..." Raina said before she could even fully wrap her head around it, "Maybe they'll be mad at first, but after some time...I think they'd understand."

Raina looked up at the unfamiliar stars, yearning to fly up there and soar until she found her way home; until she found her way back to Lucifer. As the hopelessness consumed her, there was a gentle brush against her tail. The distraction broke Raina away as she glanced down to see the stranger's own offering assistance. Without much more thought she accepted and intertwined their tails.

Down in the crater, both Azazel and Fable broke away from the rest of the group and began to make their way up the ridge as well. The sight sent a jolt of panic through Raina as she thought of the bodies. However, the stranger's gaze remained calm as he watched the two make their way up.

When they finally reached the top, Azazel crossed his arms over his chest and looked out towards the sea with a grimace. *He knew what was out there already.* Fable left the goat's side to bound over to Raina, brushing up against her like a happy cat. In turn, she leaned down to nuzzle against her companion, glad to have it back for the moment. Even if she may have to leave it.

Raina couldn't stay herself, no matter how tantalizing that idea may have been.

"I really should be on my way," Raina sighed despite not even knowing *where* she needed to go next. Fable's brows furrowed at the wording as Raina focused her attention towards the stranger, a smile on her wolf-ish face. "But I *am* really glad to have met you...What's your name?"

"Samyaza," he smiled, "and likewise, *Raina.*"

Raina nearly stumbled and the stalker flashed through her mind. She quipped, "How do you know my name?"

Samyaza looked amused at her reaction as he glanced towards Azazel, nodding the other over. The goat let out a loud and boisterous laugh that echoed around the crater.

"Lots of spirits around these parts know *you*, Raina," Azazel went on to say, tossing his arms out in a grand gesture towards the stars above. "Lucifer has been tearing up the cosmos looking for you!"

Any possible reply she had died on her tongue, and all Raina could muster was a small, "...He has?"

"While Lucifer and I don't always see eye to eye, he is admittedly a loyal spirit," Samyaza nodded as he stood up. "He must really care about you to go through such lengths."

Raina's yearning and home-sickness finally bubbled over to the point where she was a shaking mess. Lucifer had been her only friend, and his love and care had felt so genuine throughout all those years. Had she been a fool to not give him the benefit of the doubt? Truly, he *did* lie to her, but...Raina didn't care. All she wanted was to get home and just *ask* for his side of things...and if his intentions *were* bad, well...then she could figure things out from there.

"I have to go see him!" Raina sobbed, but the Watchers did not judge. "I just don't know *how* to get home!"

"You're in luck, Raina," Azazel sang with an amused smile. She blinked at him and watched as Samyaza trotted over and wrapped himself around the goat.

"We are spirits such as he," Samyaza announced, "the astral bends to *our* will, not the other way around."

He nodded at Azazel and the goat man stepped away towards the edge of the cliff. He lifted up his long clawed fingers and traced a sigil into the air, similar to the one on Raina's collar, but of a different shape.

The stars above sparkled and followed Azazel's will, the sigil appeared high up in the sky like it had been a constellation always there. And then...with a loud whoosh of air, the lines of the sigil open up. They revealed a new galaxy, one that looked much more familiar.

"While we can't get you back home," Samyaza slithered over to Raina's side and it was her turn to get wrapped around. "We can send you in the right direction."

Raina wanted to wail in joy, but could only swallow it back as she looked up at the offending portal so high above her. Shame scorned against her pelt as she whispered the truth of, "I can't fly."

Samyaza leapt from the cliff side and flapped his wings into the air, spinning around to hover only a few feet away.

"Just copy as I do," he nodded.

It was now or never.

Raina turned to Fable and it looked hopeful for the moment, until it noticed Raina's frown.

"I think this is it, Fable," her lips quivered, "it's safe here with the Watchers, probably as safe as you can get in the astral. I think it'd be a good home, if they let you stay."

Fable blinked in surprise and then looked to where Azazel stood nearby. The fallen angel shrugged, "We would always be happy to have you."

Fable glanced down at its paws before snapping its head up with enough force to make Raina flinch. There was a fire that burned within its dark eyes.

"I'll continue to travel with Raina!" Fable declared.

"A-Are you sure?" Raina stuttered, not wanting to allow her hopes to rise too much. "I...don't know what's waiting for us on the other side, if I even *have* a home for us to go back to."

"Home is just another word for Herd," Fable smiled. "And *you're* my herd now."

Quivering, Raina nodded and dipped down, lowering a wing to allow Fable to clamber up. Even if Lucifer had turned out to betray her, at least Raina had Fable. She looked towards Azazel who gave a cheeky smile and waved her off. Yes, she would also have the Watchers to turn to if she needed, and...maybe even that sea creature. Raina *wasn't* alone, not now or ever again!

With Fable safely on her shoulders, Raina braced herself against the rocks and took her first leap. She had to do it, she had to get home. Air rushed past her as she plummeted with a yelp, Fable digging its claws into her hide. The ground was never met.

Samyaza gripped Raina's shoulders before she could land amongst the Watchers again. He hoisted her up into the air as though she weighed nothing. Raina wheezed as her paws dangled through the air and then...Samyaza tossed her up ahead of him. Raina staggered and made to plummet again, but once more he caught her.

"Treat the air like you would water," Samyaza advised as he took her higher into the air, far above the mountain below. The bon-fires from there looked more like the twinkling stars above. Raina's tail twitched as Samyaza released her again, this time flapping ahead of her. The other dragon's body flowed along just like the serpent she met in the sea.

Raina flapped her wings and imagined herself fighting against the current, but...the air itself had them just as water did. Raina fell slightly, but allowed the wind to rustle her feathers as she kept her wings stretched. The flight feathers, so disused, yearned just as her heart and so she tucked to the right where there was the slightest pull upwards. The torrents caught Raina's form and boosted her up. She flapped again, a singular and hefty one, and lifted even higher.

"You're getting it, Raina!" Samyaza cheered, just as excited as she. In a fit of joy, he opened his mouth and a hot blue flame shot out in celebration. Raina was consumed by such a giddiness as Fable joined in the cheers, that she meant to blow her own flame, sparks shooting out instead. Small steps, Raina, small steps...

Samyaza kept close as the two of them made their way to Azazel's portal. His wings gave her the smallest boosts of air when she needed the extra help. When the Milky Way galaxy was in reach, Raina felt her heart tug in a different direction ever so slightly. Slowing her flapping to a hover, Raina faced the other dragon; the fallen angel.

"Samyaza!" Raina called as he came to a stop just in front of her, his wing flaps casted currents to keep her upright. Raina smiled, "Thank you for everything."

Samyaza returned it with his own and leaned forward to press his muzzle up against her forehead. In her mind's eye there was suddenly a flash of a blue colored sigil that emblazoned itself into her memories.

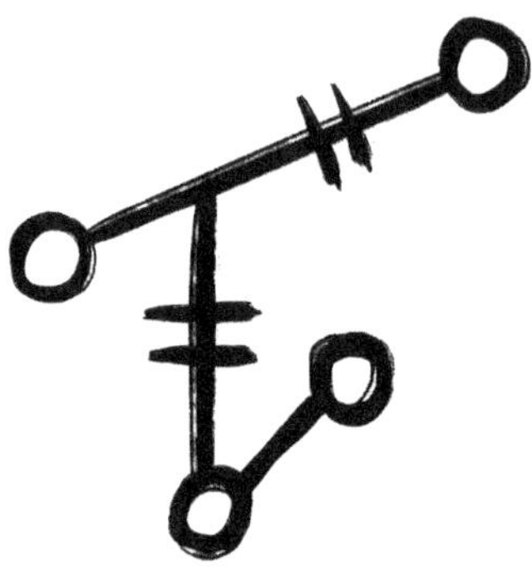

Samyaza's name echoed in her mind and she knew it to be his own. That he left the knowledge of it with her like a calling card. Samyaza leaned back and finally the two were at a distance.

"When you make it back to your body, don't be a stranger," Samyaza winked at her just before motioning her along. Raina glanced at Fable on her back, the two nodding at one another.

Feeling lighter than ever before, Raina flew through the portal, just an inch closer to home.

12

Number 36

Raina flipped out of the portal and into the open air. Fable growled and grabbed a hold of her wings pulling upwards to right the two of them into a comfortable glide. The two looked out at the galaxy before them. There were no planets Raina could see yet, nor her astral sanctuary. The space around them was practically glowing purple as Raina flew forward looking every which way for home. Home...

In a flash the light grew brighter until something appeared floating up ahead of them. Raina frowned as a strange calm came over her at the sight.

"Do we have to go back there?" Fable asked, its voice little more than a whisper.

Raina sighed, "I think we do."

Tucking her wings, she glided down towards the image of *the house*. The house where the stalker murdered her family. Raina gritted her teeth and swallowed any of the fear that tried to fight its way back. Before she could change her mind, Raina crashed through the window into the house. She flared out her wings to come to a quick stop, sliding across the sleek living room floor. Glass particles sparkled in the air as they floated around her, the hole in the side of the building allowed the purplish glow to engulf the entire house.

Something...felt different about it.

"Oh it's pretty," Fable whispered as Raina took a couple steps further into the room. Without the darkness from before, Raina could finally see the house for what it was. It was not the house of horrors she remembered, but...a home. Where her family used to roam, where they used to love.

The place had evidence of being lived in; a simmering pot on the stove, emitting the delightful scent of cinnamon and apples, and fishing poles by the front door. Raina turned towards the fireplace and not far from it was a fish tank she hadn't remembered. Inside of it was the statue of an underwater dragon, a serpent of sorts that was collecting algae. The statue was also surrounded by love, items like pretty stones and plants lovingly placed around. Under the tank on a shelf were even more trinkets, candles and seashell bowls and...an athame made to resemble coral.

Raina's jaw went slack as a realization began to spark in her mind. She didn't want to go down to the basement, but...Raina turned and headed straight towards the hallway that housed that door.

"I think I've been wrong all this time, Fable," Raina whispered. "Nobody... nobody told me."

Fable was smart and instantly picked up what Raina meant.

"Did anybody else know?" they asked, but the other wasn't sure. If her aunt *had*, then it was cruel of her to allow Raina to go on without knowing. Raina trotted into the hall and paused just as she reached the picture of her family. She looked at their smiling faces, a bit more clear, but still too blurry.

However, now the end table below the picture was perfectly visible. Raina looked down at its contents, her eye glazing over a brass statue of an angel, his arms outstretched in welcome. Raina's throat tightened as she reached over and caressed it with a gentle paw. The action sparked familiarity within her and...more love.

Had I been the fool this whole time?

Raina turned towards the basement door and Fable ducked lower to cower behind the dragon's head. Raina's heart pounded as she pushed it open. Immediately the harsh red light from before slammed into her, mixing with the purple glow to create magenta. Raina tucked her wings defensively around Fable as she took the first steps onto the basement stairs. This time she was fully in control.

As Raina made her way down, each step was colder than the last, as if she had left all warmth up in the living room. Until finally her paw pads brushed along the stony basement floor, feeling like ice. Raina looked towards the center of the room. It looked the same as before, dark and covered in blood, the image of her momma crouched in the center.

The woman, noticing the pair, looked up with her wyvern-like face, hair beginning to slide forward like tendrils. Raina slammed her paws down to show she would not be easily moved.

"You're not real!" she let out a vicious growl, "You're just an image from the past! You can't hurt me!"

The woman looked taken aback and Raina used it as her opportunity to lunge forward, her own jaws snapping. Just as she reached the woman, her momma's image vanished and with her it took the red light. Leaving Raina and Fable alone in darkness, except...Raina frowned and looked around the room as the purple glow from upstairs flowed down to fill the basement with comfort.

Raina could truly see it for what it was then.

The basement's posters shone images of the galaxies, matching well with the glow-in-the-dark stars. They reminded her of the astral and surely if they were in her own apartment, she would have loved them dearly. The couch on the other side of the room was tattered yes, but only because it had once been so thoroughly used.

Raina turned to look at the equally gnarled table. It was made from redwood to look more natural, with its legs being like roots. The deer dancing along its base were not so malicious with their sharp fangs, but were smiling in their joy. A faint memory flooded Raina's mind.

Her momma had adored that table from the day they found it abandoned on a curbside for the trashman. It had taken a lot of her father's strength to pull it all the way back to the house. Her momma loved it so much that she had turned it into the most sacred of spaces. The crystals on it surely were pricey, and arranged in a way that was pleasing to the eye. The liquid in the offering bowl had not been blood, but a thick red wine, its aroma wafting around the room.

The athame *had* been used to kill Raina's mother, but that was not its original purpose. Just as if the stalker had used a kitchen knife instead. Raina's eyes drifted from the fancy ritual knife to the owl statue and found it silly she had been so frightened of it. It was just a regular owl, except...her eyes met its own and they twinkled like the crystals themselves.

Raina looked down at where the sigil had once been on the floor, only...it was no longer there, vanished alongside the illusion of Raina's mom. She gritted her teeth; that was wrong, and at the thought, there was a bright white glow from the altar. Raina blinked and staggered over to it.

There at the feet of the owl was a shard of light and next to it, a necklace that adorned the same sigil as before. Raina knew what she had to do.

"Fable, can you hold that necklace up for me?" Raina asked as she gripped the shard of light between her teeth. Fable did as asked, and Raina trotted over to the spot where her momma had been killed.

Raina hesitated; could she really do it?

Fable, sensing her unease, nuzzled between her shoulder blades to offer up the much needed comfort. Raina looked to the shard of light and thought of Samyaza, she thought of Lucifer.

She began to draw the sigil onto the floor, just as it had been when her mother was brutally slain. Raina carefully drew out the pattern she saw on the necklace, though admittedly it was more lop-sided.

With the sigil drawn, Raina took a step back and Fable carefully slid the necklace around its own neck for safe keeping.

"So what now-" it began to say, before its voice was cut away from the room beginning to shake. Raina yelped and stumbled back as the sigil's white glow shone as bright as the sun, filling the room with warmth. The ceiling cracked and broke away, changing into a dome-shape with glass, the stars shining down on the duo; an observatory.

Raina shielded her bad eye as it stung, but couldn't look away as starlight glittered down to mingle with the sigil. There was another flash of light and then along with it came a forest of plant life and crystals that burst free from the walls. Feathers rained down and then all was still. The light eased back to the more pleasant purple and Raina could fully see that a new entity stood tall above her.

The massive owl opened their wings to reveal their melanistic barn-owl face, eyes glittering with the stars above as they took Raina in their sight. They held their head up high with an air of nobility as present in the crown of thorns on their head, mixed together with belladonna blossoms and amethyst crystals.

Despite being the one to summon them, Raina asked, "Who are you?"

"I am the thirty-sixth spirit of the Ars Goetia," responded the owl, their elegant voice came from the slight breeze that blew through the thick foliage around them. From the clank of the crystals as they clattered together. "Prince Stolas."

"*What* are you?" Raina reiterated, though she had a good inkling, as Fable nestled down between her shoulder blades, its eyes kept on Prince Stolas. The mighty owl tucked their wings finally, though their own haunted gaze never left the duo.

"I am considered a demon," they sighed, "but some think of me as a spirit of nature, such as your mother."

"So you *knew* her," Raina stated as her mouth turned dry. Prince Stolas nodded and slowly, Raina's building realization became one of horror. Prince Stolas' head dipped as a deep well of sadness overcame them.

"Your family was *pagan*, Raina," their wings sagged at the shoulders, "I was simply your mother's patron god, her teacher, her...friend."

It was all true then, Raina and everyone else had been horribly wrong about what truly transpired that night. Fable nervously patted the side of Raina's neck as a form of comfort while her tail twitched. Raina begged, "Tell me what happened...what *actually* happened."

"The story is not much different than you think, but the details are...off," Prince Stolas got out after a time. Their tone was calm, but deep within their gaze raged a geomagnetic storm. "It was a normal evening when you and Rory left for your friend's. Your mother had come down to the basement to tell me of her day, but then...we heard a commotion from upstairs and she went to go check. It was too late for your father, she found the assailant had caught him in surprise. And so she ran back down here, with the stalker having cut off all other escape. She...she managed to lock the door for a time, but his beating on it was ruthless. She prayed and prayed to me, but...I could not do anything to help her. This..."

Prince Stolas finally turned their eyes away to look up at the stars through the dome above them. A great sigh emerged from the being.

"It was not supposed to happen like this, the stars said otherwise," they explained. "She should have lived a long and good life, but...humans such as that man, only know how to blaze through the designated paths of others like wildfire."

And with that Raina was forced to wonder what her life could have looked like if even just her mother survived the attack. Would Raina have been happy then? Who would she have been? The idea of it was unfathomable and only brought a far too painful ache to her chest.

"I was honest with her that there wasn't anything I could do, but..." Prince Stolas looked back to Raina and their eyes lingered on one another. "She prayed for *your* safety instead and so I reached out to the only spirit I trusted would get the job done."

Before Raina could even think, she whispered out the name, "Lucifer..."

"Yes, as one final plea, your mother and I sent Lucifer your way," Prince Stolas explained. "He was to protect and watch over both you *and* your brother, but with the chaos of that night, he could only manage to save the one."

"Why me and not Rory?"

"I think that troublesome brother of yours made that choice himself," Prince Stolas said and their voice was sad, but rather fond. Raina let out a distraught chuckle as a white hot shame quivered down her body like a spark to a flame.

She had been so *cruel* to Lucifer during their final time together. She...she hadn't known! Lucifer's pained face flashed through her mind again and Raina nearly buckled under the weight of it. He truly *was* the same Nick that raised her; Raina should have had faith in that. During all of their interactions, they danced around the topic of her family and what had happened. Lucifer had always wanted to speak about it, but Raina...she only ever pushed him away.

Raina's thoughts went to her aunt, who was also so ready to not acknowledge the glaring elephant in the room.

"Why did everyone say she was killed as part of a ritual?" Raina gritted her teeth, "The altar items were her own!"

"The world is still such a harsh place for those of differing beliefs," Prince Stolas stepped over to the table. They trailed the tips of their wing feathers gently across the items on top of the altar. "Your parents felt it best to keep their faiths behind closed doors for fear of retribution. What if you had known and spouted at school that your mother and father worshiped demons? People could have taken you and your brother away."

"You did say the news said horrible things about Lucifer when it happened," Fable finally spoke up and without looking at it, Raina could hear the frown in its tone.

Raina nodded because she *did* finally understand what happened. The authorities had seen such Satanic-looking items in the basement and assumed the worst. For surely, Satanists and Pagans could only be awful and not in such loving families. Raina's negative feelings around the situation clawed her further open as she also thought such horrible things. Had she vented to Lucifer about it? Did she ever openly state that she hated him?

Raina felt sick and it was no wonder he had never been more honest with her. How long had Lucifer held away the hurt inside of him? Raina's throat grew thicker as her tail drooped to the floor.

"The plan was to tell you and Rory about it when you were older," Prince Stolas went on, their gaze all knowing, as if they could tell Raina's line of thought. "That way it would give you the choice on whether or not you wanted to follow down the same path."

"Prince Stolas," Raina fought to find her voice. "I'm...I'm so sorry."

"Don't be," the demon said as they took a singular stride towards her. They opened one of their wings and offered it to Raina. She hesitated, but eventually leaned forward and allowed Prince Stolas to wrap their feathers around her in a sort of hug. "Your mother loved you so dearly Raina that she would be glad that even if you wandered, you eventually found your way."

Prince Stolas' beak pressed up against the scruff of hair on top of Raina's head. With it brought a flash of memory so strong it nearly knocked her off her paws. As a child when scared or sick, her mother had also hugged her and kissed her forehead. The energy from the love pushed a burning heat down to her paws. Where the beak touched her there was a sudden sharp pain that made Raina claw at the stone floors. A scraping noise echoed around the room.

Wait...Raina opened her eyes as the pain subsided and Prince Stolas took a step back. The dragon looked down at her paws and there on each toe was a long and sharp claw, glittering like light blue diamonds.

"We're both growing horns!" Fable gasped as it pointed to the stalks on its head and then motioned towards Raina's. Slack-jawed, she reached up and was met with said horns of a similar material to that of her claws. Raina knew them to be a final gift from her mother, just as the armor on her belly was from her father.

And then with a pride Raina assumed she could have only gotten from Lucifer, she turned to Prince Stolas.

"Prince Stolas, can you help us get home?" Raina asked and so the great owl dipped their head again and turned towards the dome above them. Their wings spread out to great lengths and then the dome began to open. Several planets dotted into view and Raina gasped. Mars, Venus, Mercury and the like. Those were *her* planets, and that meant...Earth...Home.

"Carry yourself high, Raina, and be safe," is what Prince Stolas left her with as the sigil finally faded and the owl vanished.

With them gone, Raina turned to look at Fable, "Are you ready to go?"

"Are *you*?" The deer shot back and made Raina hesitate. Looking at the altar, she wondered what happened to it in the physical world, but maybe her aunt would know. Raina made a note to ask her when she got back to her body, but for now that could wait.

"Lucifer has been looking for me," Raina stated, "He's always been a bit impatient so let's not keep him waiting any longer."

Fable nodded and Raina slowly backed away from the altar, the muscles in her legs tense. Once far enough away, Raina pushed off the ground and flapped her wings to propel herself upwards. She remembered the way Samyaza's back muscles stretched with the use of his own and made sure to mirror it as best she could.

The duo flew upwards and soon the house, and its past, vanished behind them. Raina soared through the star system and past the planets she knew, but not as well as her own. Raina's good eye frantically flitted around in search of the tiny blue dot she called home when suddenly there was a light tug in her chest. She brushed a paw across the area, her claws clinking against the hard scales. Yet again there was a pull like a rope had been lassoed around her.

It was...her body! It was calling her back!

Raina pushed her wings as hard as she could to follow the direction of the pull. She was almost there, she was almost back to herself and to Lucifer, almost-

"Raina!" Fable shrieked and before her hopes could go further, a dark shadow fell over them.

13

PERSEVERANCE

R aina sensed his putrid presence far before she ever saw him, it made her fur stand on end.

"Hold on, Fable!" Raina snarled, which got the deer to do just that. Raina beat her wings to flip the two of them over, allowing her claws to lash out at the air above them. Surprised, the stalker clashed into them, all three shrieking as they tumbled through space. Raina refused to fall alone and desperately clawed at anything she could grapple with. The wyvern let out a hiss as his stretched out wings and tail were made useless by her clawing.

The two struggled against one another until something roughly caught hold of them and violently pulled them downwards. Raina yelped as frigid air stabbed through her fur, and then she slammed into the ground shortly after. A dull reddish dust puffed up around them and made it hard to breathe.

"Raina, are you alright?" Fable groaned, wincing in pain as it struggled to stand. Raina coughed as she snapped her head around. The landscape that stretched out on all sides around them was rocky and barren. Had they already made it to Earth? A haunted chill continued to blow against Raina as she felt for the tug in her chest, clinging to what little tether she had to her body. To her horror, they were no closer than before.

Raina lifted a paw to examine the red-tinted dust, were they...on Mars?

A deep growl made Raina spin around to see the stalker was laid out on the stones several feet away, beginning to stir. Raina hissed out a swear and snatched Fable up with her fangs, perhaps a bit too roughly. Fable yelped, but otherwise went slack as Raina carried it off.

A plateau jutted out of the ground not too far away and so Raina ducked behind a large rock nestled against it before she could be seen. The stalker let loose a wild and shrill call, offended that his prey had escaped once again. Raina's heart pounded painfully as she released Fable onto the ground, the deer immediately collapsed onto its side.

"You landed on me," Fable's fangs gritted as it twitched one of its back legs. "I think it's sprained."

"Damn, I'm sorry," Raina whispered as she kept her ears pricked back to listen for any advancements.

"Where are you?!" the stalker bellowed, his voice cut harshly through the quiet Mars atmosphere. His voice was so alien in this place it made Raina queasy. "Just come out! I will hunt you to the ends of reality!"

Fable's ears pinned back and it began to shake so Raina wrapped her tail around it to offer up some sort of warmth. What were they going to do? There was no way she could out fly him, and if she *did* make it back to her body? Would he just haunt her now that he had found her? Or worse, what if...what if he reached her body first?

Raina thought back to Samyaza and then Prince Stolas and the kindness they had shown her...she remembered Lucifer's adoring red eyes, looking at her like she was something to be proud of.

I'm so sorry, everyone, but...I don't think I'll be making it home today.

Raina looked from her sparkling diamond-claws to the one creature that had been her constant companion on this journey. Leaning forward she nuzzled the top of Fable's head, thankful to have had it.

"Stay here until the coast is clear," Raina whispered; she couldn't run anymore. "Then just keep running and don't look back."

"Raina-"

Raina didn't wait and leaped onto the top of the boulder. From there she could see as the stalker lashed out his claws and upturned any rock in his path; he screeched her name, looking for *her*. Despite the bubbling fear in her gut, Raina launched herself off the rock and landed hard on the cold Mars soil. Bolting right at him, dust flew up to further shield Fable from view.

Claws twitching as she neared him, the stalker whipped his head around and those haunting eyes landed right on Raina. Once more they sank into her soul, putrid and foul. Raina faltered as she slashed out her claws, only managing to graze the tip of his muzzle.

The stalker snarled and threw his massive head forward, colliding it into Raina's side. The wind was knocked from her lungs as she flew backwards through the air, landing in a heavy heap.

Heavy steps approached and Raina had to scramble to her paws. The stalker lashed out his venomous claws which clanked across Raina's chest and made her stumble back. The smaller dragon winced, waiting for the searing pain just like the wound on her face, but it never came. Shocked, Raina looked down to see there was nary a dent in the armor of her underbelly.

In defiance, Raina looked back up to the stalker, seeing him stare down the lack of injury with a flaring wrath. It made a sickening sense of pride flow through Raina's limbs.

"You can't hurt me," she snarled in the assailant's face, "not in the way you want!"

The armor had been given by her father to protect herself, and as for her mother...Raina pushed off the ground and leaped for the stalker. Her mother had given her the claws to shred his throat!

The diamonds on her paws dug into the stalker's chest, not unlike what he tried to do to her. He tossed his head back in a shriek and stumbled, the first hints of a rust-colored blood beading at the wounds. Raina's eyes locked onto it, his skin was tough, but not so much that she couldn't cut it open.

So she went for him again, but this time he was prepared and knocked her back with a heavy hit from one of his wings. Raina tried to leap back up, but the stalker crashed down on top of her back, rolling her over with ease to pin her wings.

Raina barred her teeth and shoved her paws into his chest. He wasn't so much bigger than her like when they first met in the asteroid field. Yet still Raina had to strain her muscles to keep the stalker's snapping fangs away from her face.

"Get off! Get off!"

An inhuman wail sailed through the Mars air as something small and brown collided with the stalker's face, making him stagger off. Fable howled as it clawed and kicked with all its might, marring the hideous face of the wyvern. Raina's muscles locked with a flash of memory. *A young boy pushed her to the door as he turned to face his much larger opponent.*

The stalker reared up with a pained bellow that snapped Raina back to reality and so she kicked her back legs into his. The stalker fell backwards and lashed out his wings, striking Fable in the side. The deer collided roughly with the ground a few feet away just as the stalker whipped his tail out to regain balance.

"Ror- Fable!" Raina called out as the stalker turned his attention to where the little deer lay sprawled out. "Don't you hurt it!"

"You say that as if its pain isn't your own fault," the stalker huffed as he looked back at Raina in disgust. "Just like when you selfishly left your brother to die. Women like you never want to be held accountable for your actions."

"I was a *child*!" a white hot anger shot through Raina as she pulled herself up to standing, her eyes locked onto the stalker's. "And what about *you*, people like *you* only know how to hurt others! You think your cruelty separates you, but...your lack of empathy will be your downfall..."

"The only thing I regret is that I didn't kill you that night," the stalker chuckled, making Raina burn even hotter as she stepped between the stalker and Fable. Her tail lashed out, how dare he- how *dare* he!

"You *did* kill me that night," Raina stood up straight, gnashing her teeth at the other dragon. "The Raina that I used to be...but *this* Raina is here now to make sure you stay dead!"

The stalker had the audacity to look amused at that; he never had taken her seriously had he? Before he could utter anymore of his venom, Raina leaped at him without warning. Their bodies collided and Raina's teeth found their way around his long and spindly throat. They crushed through his scales like a June bug and Raina gagged as congealed blood hit her tongue. Still she did not let go as the stalker let out a frenzied and gurgled scream, blood filling his own mouth.

The two of them collapsed into the dusty ground, writhing as their claws slashed and cut at one another. The stalker's aim was reckless and desperate as he tried to wrench Raina off, but even as painful claws sliced at her legs and shoulders, she held true. Raina opened her mouth, meaning to chomp back down again, but the stalker used it as an opportunity to shove her away. He went to leap on top of her again and Raina whipped her head down.

The stalker landed on top of her...right on her diamond-sharp horns. They went straight through his soft underbelly, for the stalker no longer had anyone that loved him enough to shield his form. The monster wheezed, eyes bulged wide, and then Raina pushed her head up into his gut even harder. A sickening goo splattered down her horns and around her face. The stalker writhed and slapped his wings onto her back in attempt to wrench himself off. The limbs quivered, void of the strength they once had, and then...

The stalker grew still. Raina shoved him off and the wyvern landed with a heavy thud. Panting, Raina stared at him, not quite believing the strange sense of surrealism that overcame her. Still, she had more pressing matters.

Not giving the stalker the time of day, Raina hurried away from him, over to Fable's side.

"Are you alright?!" she gasped just as the deer lifted up its head, a little wobbly.

"I-I think so," Fable dragged itself up, though its sprained leg pulled behind it had an awkward angle. Raina winced as she wrapped her body around the other, using her side to help support it.

"Come on, let's get out-" Raina and Fable both froze as a wheeze sounded out across from them. The stalker's body twitched and spasmed. You had to be kidding! Why wouldn't he stay dead?! Raina barred her bloody fangs again as she hovered defensively over Fable. It didn't matter, she would kill him as many times as she needed to!

The stalker dragged himself up, head hung limply on its twisted neck as those soulless eyes bared down on her. Toxins leaked from his ridged scales, mixed in with the dark blood that poured from his belly. He staggered towards her with a wheeze, mouth opened to spout something unintelligible. Raina's fur stood on end as she began to worry if he could even *be* killed again. Legs shaking, she braced herself for another fight that would never come.

For the stalker reached out for her with his clawed wings and then there was a flash. A heavy slam on the Mars ground that made a thick cloud of red dust swirl up into the air. Raina's eyes were wide, her jaw slack, as they were met with a wall of flurrying feathers. Massive black wings shielded her view from the stalker.

"Disgusting parasite," the man before her said as he reached out an elegant hand to brush it along the stalker's snout. The creature looked at the man in horror, eyes nearly bulging as his scales started to peel away and fall from his body. Right before Raina's eyes, the stalker that had hunted and tormented her fell to pieces, turning to a harmless dust. Never again to hurt her or anyone else.

The winged man gave a singular powerful flap and the dust that was once the stalker blew away. It swirled up into the atmosphere of space, never to be whole again.

Raina carefully stepped back as the man turned to peer at her through his long curtain of dark hair, his red eyes vibrant and striking.

Lucifer.

14

THE DRAGON AND THE DEVIL

The real, *actual* Lucifer.

Raina's mouth went dry as anything she could have possibly said left her brain. The demon stood there and looked directly at her now as he turned away from whatever husk was left of the stalker. As if the creature was nothing compared to him and his own power; and Raina knew that to be true. A chilled Mars wind blew against the small group, which made Raina's fur fluff up.

"You've grown so much, Raina," Lucifer went on to say, as if just to say *something*. The dragon realized it was true for she stood at eye level with him now, just as tall and proud as he. Though currently...he looked anything but. Lucifer's scarlet eyes were full of a deep sadness that he seldom ever let her see before, the look sparking something in Raina's brain.

"I've...been through a lot," Raina stated, though perhaps that would have been an understatement. Oh to tell her old friend of all she had seen and done.

"You're still wearing the necklace," Lucifer commented instead, his eyes flicked over the golden collar and maybe...just maybe he also sought out their past connection.

Raina frowned, "I am."

Taking it off had never been a thought to cross her mind. Perhaps she knew deep down, or maybe just desperately hoped that Lucifer was truly the same Nick he always had been.

And as the last of her fears and concerns still tried to linger, Raina had to ask, "How did you find me here?" Because what if it *all* had still been a sham?

"Dearest, dear of my heart, the moment you went through that portal, I went looking all over for you!" Lucifer let out a loud sigh, his exhaustion showed through the way his shoulders sagged. And Raina couldn't suppress her fond smile as the demon tossed his arms up in exaggeration. "I sought out every demon, angel and god I knew of that specialized in finding lost things, but none of them could even get a trace of you. I shouted my woes to all who would listen! It was only a bit ago that Leviathan told me they found you and left you at Mount Hermon. I rushed over so quickly, but you had already gone and those blasted Watchers were hardly any help! But Samyaza did eventually tell me they led you to Stolas, who told me you were on your way home! What a dilemma this all has been!"

And Raina couldn't help the small chuckle that escaped her. It would seem that Lucifer had quite the journey himself. At the sound of her laughter, said demon grew very still as he took her in his sights. Lucifer absentmindedly played with his fingers, something she noticed he did when he was too nervous to say something.

"Listen, my child," he whispered, and Raina's heartbeat picked up. His words sounded final, like a good-bye. "I'll understand if you hate me now-"

Raina slammed into Lucifer, making the demon let out a gasp, but he nary even stumbled back. For Raina it felt like she collided with a rock as she desperately pawed at his back. Like she was trying to encompass her guardian's entire being into a wanting hug. She gnashed her fangs and lashed her tail, no longer caring as she buried her much larger head into his shoulder, getting a face full of feathers.

"L-Lucifer!" Raina wailed, the first of her tears cascaded down her face. She sniffled and noted how the wings had the slight smell of smoke. Not at all like the desolation of a house fire like the stalker had, but something more pleasant. Smores on a campfire, a freshly blown out candle. Raina sputtered, "I-I missed you so much! I was s-s-so scared!"

Lucifer wrapped his arms around her as well as he could, without question, and for the first time she truly noticed the strength within them. She was a dragon, yes, but he was truly something else. Not a human ghost, but a god in his own right. *Light bringer, the knowledge giver, lover of the arts and music.* These words passed through Raina's mind as if the touch between them had allowed Lucifer to let her know who he truly was. There was no question as to why her mother would ask such a spirit to watch over her children. Raina could sense her hot shame, and hated how she initially reacted to finding out who he was.

"I'm sorry," Raina began as she tried to hold him tighter, but Lucifer gently removed her so he could lean back and get a better view of her face. His eyes immediately snapped to the wound over her left eye, lip twitching as if he fought off against a sneer. Instead, Lucifer kept his cool and gently brushed his fingers across the pink scars.

"Don't be," he said with a sigh that held the weight of the world on his shoulders. "I should have been far more honest with you sooner. I just...feared losing you, but I know that wasn't fair to you."

Raina wanted to argue, but she found there was no point in it. So instead she let out a chuckle and whispered, "I guess both of us have made a lot of mistakes, huh?"

His lips pursed, Lucifer took a moment to think that over before he finally nodded in agreement.

"Can...Can we start over?" Raina attempted, though she didn't know if they were too far gone to accomplish such a thing. However...she still loved Lucifer with all her heart and it was something she *needed* to try. And as a sad smile appeared on his face, she knew he did as well.

"I would like that," Lucifer whispered and so Raina nodded.

"Hello, I'm Raina, I've...been through a lot in life," she got out, even as the familiar pull of hesitation plucked at her heart. She couldn't hide from it any longer, they *had* to talk about it. "My family was killed by my best friend's brother, he was stalking me and I didn't know it at the time. I was...I was only ten years old...I'm very lonely and still incredibly in pain, but I want help to improve my life from here on out."

"Greetings, dear Raina, I am Lord Lucifer," the demon said as he sat his hand over his own heart; an oath. "I reign over the air and Venus, the direction East. I adore helping people find their paths in life and so I would be honored to be your patron deity, if you'd have me."

Raina nodded despite not exactly knowing all of what that would entail, but she would have so many more years with Lucifer to figure it out. Raina thought about what her mother's relationship with Prince Stolas was like and hoped for the same. She thought of the altar table and hurriedly looked around her paws until she spotted a perfectly round Mars rock.

"O-Oh, um!" she snagged it and lifted it up towards him, her first *official* offering. "Here, have this!"

Lucifer blinked in surprise as he stared at the rock, making Raina's face heat up. How silly she was to think any old rock would be sufficient for an entity as old as he. Raina was about to back track when a genuine smile appeared on Lucifer's face. He cupped his hands and accepted the stone as if it were as precious as any crystal. Eyes sparkling, he said, "I will treasure it always."

"I don't know if I've ever said it," Raina said as Lucifer slipped the rock into his robes, "but you have meant the world to me, Lucifer, and I don't think I would have lasted as long as I did without you. You're my family, and I love you."

"I love you too, dear Raina," Lucifer reached out and sat his hand on top of her head just as he always did. That's when Raina truly knew they would be fine. It would still be difficult, she was sure, but as long as they had each other she could keep on her own two feet... or sometimes, four paws.

"Um, so is everything okay now, or..." came the voice of Fable as it peeked out from behind Raina, wide eyes locked onto Lucifer. Raina blinked in shock; Fable had been so quiet so she could have her reunion with Lucifer.

"Oh, an astral creature!" Lucifer exclaimed, eyes narrowing at Fable. Raina remembered Lucifer's warnings about dangerous astral entities and quickly cast a wing over her smaller companion.

"It's my friend!" Raina exclaimed, "I wouldn't have made it back without it."

Lucifer hummed in contemplation as he scanned the deer-like creature over. Fable nervously shifted on its paws and mumbled out a, "Er, nice to meet you Lord Lucifer, I am Fable of Story's End."

That appeared to have the desired effect as Lucifer smiled.

"While I normally wouldn't allow a possibly unpredictable entity to hang around," he said, "I'll make an exception this time, it's nice to meet you Fable of Story's End."

The demon walked around Raina and stooped down to offer a hand to the critter. Fable smiled and sat back on their haunches to lift a paw. The two shook on it and Raina was able to let out a breath of relief.

"So what now?" Raina asked as Lucifer carefully scooped Fable up into his arms, being careful of their injured leg. Both of them turned their heads to look at Raina and the sight flooded her with warmth; her family.

"I would say we should have a picnic! I simply *must* hear about your journey," Lucifer began before his brows furrowed, "but...how about I take Fable to your astral home and show them around while you go get an *actual* meal?"

And for the first time ever, Raina whispered, "I'd really like that, actually..."

Raina's eyes snapped open with a sharp gasp, her body vibrating as her astral form nestled itself back inside. Just as if she had never truly been gone. The image of her dark and stained ceiling came into view as her eyes adjusted. Sitting straight up, she nearly fell back down as everything rushed to her head. Woozy, she looked at the clock beside her bed and...Only fifteen minutes had passed.

Still though, Raina felt like she hadn't slept, drank, or eaten in days. Her ravenous stomach clawed at her and so Raina tossed her legs over the side of her bed. Thinking back to her journey, Raina frowned as the earliest of it was already beginning to grow fuzzy.

Leaping into action, Raina grabbed a notebook and pencil from her night-stand before she rushed into the kitchen. She grabbed another cup of noodles and sensed the age-old sensation of Nick's incorporeal form approaching her, though now she knew it to truly be Lucifer's energy. It was slightly different now, more solid, as he no longer had secrets to keep. Raina frowned down at the cup of noodles.

"Maybe I'll try to buy something different tomorrow," Raina commented as she tossed the cup into the microwave. Change would take time.

With the noodles heating up in the microwave, Raina sat at her tiny kitchen table where her previous meal still sat abandoned and opened the notebook. She began to write in great detail what had happened. Lucifer stepped closer and

Raina smiled as she accepted his energy to be near. Then she felt a second smaller presence enter the room and curiously look around. Raina grinned; Fable.

And then she began her tale.

"So after I got sucked up into the blackhole, I ended up in a redwoods forest-"

15

Dragons of a Feather

The small and cluttered shop was like a second home to her now as she stepped over and pilfered through the candles. She picked up two large pillar ones, a green and a red. Perhaps carving sigils into them would be a perfect offering, she imagined. Raina smiled and made her way towards the small metaphysical shop's cash register, where Samantha was discreetly trying to use their phone.

'Do we really have the room for that now?' Lucifer's voice bounced around her head. Raina withheld a chuckle at the demon's exasperated huff, however playful it was.

"I wanted to get them before I forget, they'll fit in the moving boxes," Raina thought back to him as Samantha smiled at her and began to type the candle prices onto their computer. Raina thumbed at the carnelian necklace she wore, a habit she picked up whenever she grew too nervous. It was a sort of way to feel more of Lucifer's presence in a physical sense, for the necklace was one she wore in honor of him. She had even managed to paint his sigil on it in gold, a way to represent her dragon collar while in the physical world. Though Raina wondered if she could add some sort of serpentine piece of jewelry here soon. Just as she had already added an antique bracelet with a small deer charm on it. She never went anywhere without wearing them. Raina chuckled, *"Besides when I get the table set up, there'll be enough room for the both of you."*

A flash of excitement shot through Raina's belly as Samantha handed off her bag. She smiled and mumbled a quick thanks, but it was soon dashed as Samantha's eyes flicked down straight to the necklace. Their gaze eyed the sigil, and then asked, "Isn't that Lucifer's?"

Raina tried not to choke because she had been initially anxious to add the sigil to her necklace and now her fears were a reality...Now, perhaps she would be ostracized before she even started and would no longer be able to go to that shop. Raina cleared her throat as she felt Lucifer's reassurance against her. It helped to quell her invasive thoughts.

"Um, yeah, he's my patron," Raina admitted, for even if she was nervous, she would *never* be ashamed of that fact. She would never hide it, no matter how scary things could be.

"Oh, cool," Samantha nodded, "I hear he's a really great spirit to work with. I'm a Hellenic pagan, myself. Zeus and all that."

"I've never met another pagan before," Raina commented as she held the bag of candles to her chest. The thought relieved her, even if their particular beliefs weren't exactly the same.

"Well you better get used to it," Samantha chuckled before their head tilted to the side. "When do you start anyway?"

"Next week," Raina nodded, "it would have been sooner, but I'm super busy with the move."

"Right, right."

And with that the two bid each other a farewell. Though it would only be until Raina started her new job at that very shop in the coming weeks. Raina hurried from the building and out onto the street, though the sudden flash of sunlight made her wince. As her left eye watered, she found she didn't mind it. It was evidence that what she had gone through in the astral was real. Raina felt more at ease, but was eager to return to the safety of her temporary apartment. The candles were heavy in her arms and she couldn't hold in her excitement at the idea of placing them proudly on her own altar...She only had to wait until she was in the new house.

Raina thought about her momma's table and how worried she was that it had been thrown away. When she contacted her aunt after her astral mishap a few weeks back, she was overjoyed to learn that a lot of her family's belongings had been placed in storage. Waiting until Raina was ready to accept them, a fact that made her sob.

The athame, of course, had been put into evidence and was long gone. Not that Raina wanted it anyway, she would get her own. Most of the other altar items were gone as well, which was fine. Raina would start anew.

Lucifer, picked up her thoughts, and kept things light as he also thought about the beautiful table. He huffed, *'Why do I have to share it with him, though,* **I'm** *your patron!'*

"I'm allowed to connect with more spirits other than just you, ya know, I already do," Raina chuckled as she continued on her way.

'Yes, but **DEERest** *Fable doesn't boss us around like Samyaza will!'* Lucifer continued on, not exactly a fan of incorporating more entities into their little spiritual family. *'Just you wait!'*

"Well, if anyone gets a little too in their own head, they'll get put on the end table for a bit."

'I suppose that'll suffice.'

The love that filled Raina soon fell away as she passed by the games shop. Coming to a stop, she looked through the glass, noting the same party of gamers at their table. Raina looked down at the trinkets lining the window, miniatures and statues of fantastical creatures.

She wondered if they had any angel ones. Raina would love to get a statue for Lucifer just as her mother had for Prince Stolas, even if it wasn't quite as extravagant. There *was* the possibility of using the one that had been in her family's hallway, but Raina yearned for her own.

Raina took a deep breath, thumbed the necklace, and entered the building. The door's bell dinged and made her tense, but only one person at the table glanced over before returning to their game. That was fine, that was nothing compared to the Watchers' hundreds of eyes staring her down.

Raina made her way over to a wall filled with plastic statues and figures, scanning over each one for any that could resemble Lucifer. However, she didn't find a single one and so she would continue on her search. Her current favorite place to find items to use in her pagan practice was a local antique store. They hadn't gotten any angel statues that weren't super cutesy yet, but the owner promised to keep an eye out for her.

'Oh, Raina, turn around!' Lucifer said and as she did, came face to face with a swiveling wrack full of stuffed animals. The one in front of her being a deer. Lucifer seemed amused, *'Other than the lack of paws and fangs, it's a spitting image of our little friend, don't you think?'*

It was. Raina smiled and collected the thing into her arms along with the candle bag; might as well not leave empty handed after-all. Raina took the deer plush to the counter to pay and as the cashier rang it up, she listened to the group behind her cheer after some successful dice roll. Raina accepted the deer plushie back and turned to look at the table.

"Maybe Viola will want to get into table-tops," Raina commented. "Her parents never let her do stuff like that, but I've always wanted to try."

'I'm sure she would be down for that,' Lucifer said. *'She was okay with having me around, after all.'*

Raina nodded with a fondness for her childhood friend. It was a miracle that the two of them had even crossed paths again. Though Raina suspected that the meeting might have been set up between Lucifer and Viola's guardian angel. It had been an awkward interaction and Raina nearly had a panic attack upon seeing Viola's eyes, so similar to her brother's, but that was neither here nor there.

Viola had been hurt too, Raina came to realize, and now they were going to heal together.

"I think it'll be good for us," Raina took a careful step towards the table, "but I don't know how to play..."

Without much thought and feeling like Lucifer gently pushed on her back to urge her forward, Raina approached the table. Each person from the group looked up at her as she clutched the plush for dear life. *Deer* life as Lucifer would joke.

"H-Hey, could I watch?" she asked, tongue far too dry. "I want to learn how to play."

The group looked to a single man at the head of the table, most of the supplies surrounding him. Raina was knowledgeable enough to know he must have been the Game Master, or whatever they were called. The man just smiled at her and motioned to an empty chair.

"The more the merrier," he said, "just don't backseat-game."

Soon the group went back to their strategizing as if all was well. Raina let out a breath of relief as she stepped over to the chair to sit down without issue. As if she was one of them, Raina smiled and sat her deer plushie on the edge of the table where it wouldn't be in the way.

"Who's your little friend there?" the girl beside her asked, likely trying to ease whatever was left of the awkward air.

"It's Fable, I think," Raina chuckled, figuring she might as well use the plush as a link to her astral companion. No one said she *couldn't* do that. At the dubbing of the name, the plushy grew a new air about it and Raina could practically hear the clop of hooves as Fable curiously entered the room. Unseen and unfelt by those who did not know it.

And the little astral family stayed there for a few hours, simply watching the game be played, learning about it. Occasionally Raina would have light conversations with the group. She would learn and she would make friends. Raina would decide to join their gaming group, especially since she was only moving thirty-six minutes away with Viola.

It was a small house but it would be theirs. They would be safe to express themselves how they wanted and live their lives to their fullest. The shackles of the past loosened enough that Raina knew this to be true. She was free, even if it was always going to be a constant uphill journey for her.

Even if she wasn't physically a dragon, mentally she was, and she was also just as strong as one. As strong as she had ever been with Lucifer and Fable of Story's End by her side.

Now and forever, until Raina would take her final breath, and even beyond that.

ABOUT THE AUTHOR

Riley Daemon is a proud pagan with a deep love for the demonic. They showcase this passion by making art and writing about witchcraft and the occult. Riley adores wolves and owls, but ultimately is a cat person.

Also by Riley Daemon

Stand Alone Novels

Whispers in the Forest

Astral Stalker

Series

Bringing Forth Belial

Book 1- *Bringing Forth Belial*

Other Works

A Love Letter to the Devil- Short non-fiction story featured in *Reverent: An Anthology of Divinity*

The Devil Ain't So Bad- Free to read 14k word short story

All can be found through rileydaemon.com or other online retailers!